HIS LOST WIFE

A psychological thriller novella

A J WILLS

Cherry Tree
Publishing

Chapter 1

'Excuse me. Hello? Can you hear me?'

As I peeled open my eyes, my head lolling forwards and a cricked muscle in my neck complaining, I stared into the dark eyes of an unfamiliar face. A man was crouching in front of me, frowning behind a pair of heavy-rimmed glasses. He had an impressive head of jet-black hair swept neatly into a side parting and was dressed casually in a checked blue shirt and linen trousers. The quiet hum of an early morning crowd buzzed in my ears.

'Are you okay? You're bleeding.' The man nodded at my temple.

I instinctively raised a hand to touch my head and found I was clutching a tissue crusted with dried blood. I dabbed my skin and winced at a sharp stab of pain, the tenderness of a rising bruise suggesting I must have tripped or fallen and smacked my skull hard. I glared at the fresh crimson smear on the tissue with no idea what I'd done.

'Where am I?' I asked, confused, my eyes struggling to focus. Certainly not at home in my bed.

As the man narrowed his eyes, a soft, warm hand touched my wrist, making me jolt. A woman was sitting on the edge of the seat next to me, her knees angled in my direction and concern etched on her face. The man's wife? She had the same dark skin and hair as black as a raven's wing, scraped away from her forehead and held in place behind a navy velvet band. She smelled of vanilla and smudges of smoky charcoal make-up gave the impression her eyes were sunk deep into their sockets. On the next seats along, two young girls I assumed were their children were concentrating on their mobile phones, swinging their legs, totally disinterested in me.

'You're at the airport,' the man said, worry lines creasing his brow. 'Don't you remember?'

As he crouched, holding his balance with three fingertips on the ground, his thigh muscles bulged. Through a scratched clear screen behind him, I looked onto a cavernous concourse below, surrounded by shops, a money exchange bureau and the exit to a train station where a straggle of tired-looking people tramped through in a quiet daze.

'The airport?' I plumbed the depths of my mind, trying to remember what I was doing there.

'Gatwick,' the man confirmed. 'Do you have a flight to catch?'

'What? No.' I sat up and rolled my neck, easing the tightness around my shoulders. At least I didn't think I did. 'What time is it?'

With a grimace, the man stood and checked a gold watch on his wrist. 'Just gone seven,' he said. 'Have you been here all night?'

Had I? I couldn't remember. In fact, what was the last thing I did remember? Everything was so foggy and confused, my thoughts and memories tumbling over themselves in a hazy jumble.

'Can you remember what you did to your head?' the woman asked when I didn't answer. She spoke in a slow, raised voice as if she was talking to a child.

'I must have slipped.' I touched the wound again. Another spot of blood seeped into the tissue, but it didn't seem too bad.

'You probably ought to get it looked at. Are you here with anyone?'

My spirits soared. 'My wife,' I gasped. 'Ruby!'

'Do you know where she is?'

I glanced around at the rows of vinyl seats littered with people waiting for flights in a narrow space squeezed in between a shop and a restaurant. There were bodies everywhere, of all ages and nationalities. People in transit, waiting for flights or to meet loved ones. Some slumped in their seats looking at their phones, others laid out horizontally, sleeping with their heads on rolled up jumpers and coats.

But I couldn't see Ruby anywhere.

Panic gripped my chest.

Maybe she'd gone to grab a coffee or visit the bathroom and had slipped away, not wanting to wake me. She'd be back soon. She wouldn't have left me here, would she?

'That cut looks really nasty. We should take him to get it seen by someone,' the woman said to her husband.

The man grunted. 'We don't have time. We need to go.'

'We can't leave him here.'

They were talking about me like I wasn't there, a child who didn't know his own mind.

'I'm fine,' I said, trying to stand, but a rush of blood sent my head spinning. The ground beneath my feet felt like it was dropping away as if I was in an elevator, free falling from the top of a towering skyscraper.

When was the last time I'd seen Ruby?

On the plane?

In the airport in Rome?

The last memory I had was dancing with her under the stars on a balmy night in the Piazza Barberini, a little drunk but happier than I could ever remember. She was wearing the sleeveless black dress I'd surprised her with as a honeymoon gift. It suited her perfectly, making her look like a blonde Audrey Hepburn, a vision of elegance and grace.

'Don't try to get up,' the woman said, clutching my elbow as I slumped back into my seat. 'You might be concussed.'

'I'm fine,' I said. 'I just need to find my wife.'

'I'm sure she's here somewhere.' The man glanced up at a TV screen on the wall listing the arrivals and departures to and from far-flung destinations. 'What's your name?'

'Victor,' I said. 'Victor Cano.'

'Do you have your wife's number? We could try calling her,' the woman suggested.

I shook my head. A painful explosion ripped through my skull and an eruption of bright lights flashed behind my eyes. 'She doesn't have a phone,' I said, sickness broiling in my gut.

'Oh, right.' I'm not sure she believed me.

'I'm sorry, I really have to go,' I said, easing myself up onto my feet.

'Why don't you wait here with us until we can find someone to help you?' The man snatched my arm as I struggled to find my balance.

I shrugged his hand away. 'I told you, I'm fine. I just need to find Ruby.'

'Take it easy, Victor.' He withdrew his hand, but I didn't like the familiar way he used my name. I didn't know him from Adam.

'I'll stay here with him and you see if you can find someone,' the woman said to her husband.

I sighed. I wished they could take a hint. 'Thank you for your kindness, but I have to go,' I said. 'I have to find Ruby.'

The guy looked at me over the top of his glasses. 'Look, Victor, you have a head injury. Someone needs to take a look at you. Sangeeta will stay with you. I'll be as quick as I can.'

'No,' I said, raising my voice. 'I appreciate your concern, but I'm perfectly alright. Please, don't make a fuss.'

'But -'

'I'd hate for you to miss your flight,' I said. 'Are you going somewhere nice?'

'Minorca,' they replied in unison.

I nodded, although I'd never been.

'Two weeks,' the man added. 'We can't wait.'

'I hope you have a wonderful time.' I squeezed between them as he shrugged at her and she mouthed something at him I didn't catch.

'Victor, listen to me,' the man said, but I was already walking away with my head down and my hands dug into my pockets, fighting against a swell of people moving in the opposite direction towards the departure gates, like salmon heading upstream. Some were wheeling small bags behind them. Others had rucksacks slung over their shoulders. But it occurred to me I was empty-handed. I didn't have a bag or a case, which was odd. I'm sure we would have had luggage if we'd flown in from Rome the previous night.

So where were our cases?

And more importantly, where the hell was Ruby?

Chapter 2

I scanned both ways in the desperate hope of spotting Ruby somewhere among all the people. Then wandered past a newsagent where the earthy smell of newspaper print mingled with a waft of cheap, sweet perfume, and a coffee shop where a long queue waited patiently while two harassed-looking baristas were struggling to cope with the rush. I checked behind pillars and pockets of seating areas. But I couldn't see Ruby anywhere. I glanced down the escalators and stairs delivering people to the upper floor departure gates and finally found myself at a dead end next to a chapel and prayer room. I doubted Ruby would be in there. Although she believed in God, she'd never been religious.

She must be somewhere, though, but the airport was so big. What if she'd become disorientated and got lost? Or forgotten where she'd left me sleeping? What if she had returned, found that I'd gone and now we were both wandering around trying to find each other like two ships lost in the fog?

We'd been inseparable for the last week. Ruby had rarely been out of my sight as we'd become absorbed in each other's lives, learning each other's tics and habits. Like the fact Ruby always cleaned her teeth for exactly two minutes, every morning after breakfast and the last thing before bed, concentrating first on the right side of her mouth and then the left. That she had a tiny birthmark on her shoulder blade the shape of North America. That she preferred to sleep on the left side of the bed and always laid out the clothes she was going to wear the next day on a chair the night before. That she avoided the cracks in the pavement for luck - a habit she said she'd developed as a child - and that she needed to close all the wardrobe doors and drawers before she could sleep.

The wedding had been stressful and tiring, although more so for Ruby than for me. All I'd had to do was turn up on time and not fluff my vows. But Ruby had treated the day like she was planning a military operation, overseeing every tiny detail, from the flowers in the church to the design of the bridesmaids' dresses. She'd wanted it to be perfect - and it was - but it had consumed so much of her energies that I was glad when it was over and I finally had her all to myself again.

My responsibility was the honeymoon. I considered Paris, the city of lovers, but decided it was a cliche. As was Venice. But Rome, with its beautiful historic architecture, cobblestone streets and ancient monuments, would be ideal. It helped that Ruby's father insisted on paying for the hotel.

And for his little girl, only the best would do. The grandeur and opulence of the St Regis on the Via Vittorio Emanuele Orlando in the heart of historic Rome was out of this world. They'd treated us like royalty from the moment we arrived, with champagne on ice in our room and rose petals showered over pristine white bedsheets. I'd never felt so pampered. And I got to share it with the woman of my dreams.

We spent the week with our heads in the clouds, intoxicated on each other's love. And to think it was all down to a random one-in-a-billion chance encounter that we'd met at all. In truth, it was lucky I hadn't killed her. Instead, I took her to lunch, and we never looked back.

Rome had been amazing. It turned out to be an excellent choice for our honeymoon. We'd had our picture taken sitting on the Spanish Steps, tossed coins into the Trevi Fountain, and marvelled at the majesty of the Colosseum. And when our feet were aching and our stomachs rumbling, we'd taken refuge in street cafes and restaurants, drinking strong espressos, and eating pizza and pasta washed down with fine bottles of chianti. In the evenings, we drank negronis and wandered hand-in-hand through sparkling piazzas buzzing with nightlife. It was the best time of my life. But it had flashed by in a heartbeat.

The last image I could remember was Ruby in that beautiful black dress, with tears of laughter streaming down her cheeks, as we strolled back to the hotel, drunk and in love. I couldn't remember getting back to the hotel. Nor packing or taking a taxi to the airport the next morning. The flight. The landing. Stepping back onto home soil. Or following the signs to reclaim our baggage. It was all gone. The memories simply weren't there.

I dabbed my head with the tissue again. It was still bleeding a little and sore to the touch. I must have fallen hard. Maybe even knocked myself out. God knows how. Maybe I *was* concussed. It would explain my memory loss at least. But it didn't explain why Ruby was missing.

With my heart beating fast in my chest, I hurried back towards the seats where I'd been woken by the dark-haired couple.

'Ruby?' I muttered under my breath, my lungs struggling as I marched through a sea of strangers. 'Ruby?'

A young man wearing a pair of headphones clamped over his ears, eyes down, grazed my shoulder as I squeezed past him, knocking us both off our stride.

He glanced back and held up an apologetic hand.

I pushed on. Ruby had to be here somewhere. Where else could she be? But a niggling doubt gnawed in my gut. I feared that something had happened to her, that she was in real danger and needed my help. A sweaty dew broke out across my forehead as a hot flush prickled my skin. What was I going to do?

My breath became ragged and my legs suddenly felt as weak as water. I stepped to one side, almost tripping over a wheeled flight bag a young woman was hauling behind her and rested against a wall with my head buried into my forearm, trying to get my breath back. I took a deep lungful of air and let it out slowly, attempting to pacify my racing mind. If I was going to find Ruby, I needed to keep a straight head. There was no point in panicking.

But I was becoming increasingly convinced that something bad had happened to her. She wouldn't have just left me. If only I could remember the last twenty-four hours and how we'd become separated. But my mind remained a blank. A black hole. Did it have something to do with the bump on my head? Was it connected to our missing luggage? And why did I have the feeling we were running from something or someone? Was it just the dark claw of paranoia or a genuine memory fighting to be remembered?

A hand clamped onto my shoulder, and I flinched.

'Hey,' said a voice in my ear.

Every muscle in my body tightened, fear spiking through my veins, and I span around with my fists clenched, ready to fight.

Chapter 3

Ruby ran a slender finger under her eyelid, lifting a fake lash to hook out a mote of dust. She blinked, her eyes watering, and sneezed.

'Are you coming down with something?' Yolanda asked, emerging from the stockroom laden with a pile of shoeboxes.

'Something in my eye, that's all.'

Ruby blinked four more times until the sting subsided, then returned her attention to the row of dresses she was rearranging on the rail in the trendy Knightsbridge boutique where she worked. She didn't need the money, but she liked to be independent and show her parents she could stand on her own two feet. Besides, it was only for two days a week, and apart from the one day she helped at a women's refuge, the rest of the week was her own.

Yolanda dumped the boxes on the floor with a groan. 'Seeing Hugo tonight?'

Ruby turned up her nose. 'He wants to take me out for dinner again,' she said.

'Lucky girl.'

'If I'm honest, I'd rather stay in.'

'Are you going cold on him?' Yolanda lowered herself to her knees, adjusting her skirt around her thighs, and sat back on her heels.

'I don't know. He's very nice ...'

'But?'

'It's hard to explain,' Ruby said, plucking a sheath dress off the rail and smoothing down the fabric.

'You're not that into him?'

'I mean, he's lovely and everything, but you know, I find him a bit ...' Ruby rolled her eyes up towards the fake crystal chandelier Yolanda had installed to lend the boutique a bit of class. 'Suffocating.'

'What do you mean?'

'I'm still so young but he's talking about marriage and kids and settling down and I'm really not sure I'm ready for all of that.'

'Not ready for it? Or not ready for it with Hugo?'

'I don't know. Of course, it doesn't help that Daddy thinks the world of him.'

'Sure he does. But I'm sure he'd feel the same if any duke or earl with a few pennies to rub together took a shine to his daughter.'

Ruby looked aghast. 'Yolanda! Don't say that.'

She laughed. 'Why? It's true. And you know it.'

'Isn't,' she said, but in her heart she knew Yolanda was right.

Her father was smitten with Hugo Nightingale because of his heritage. He was the son of the Earl of Ruttingham and stood to inherit not only his father's title on his death, but his sprawling estate in Dorset. If she married him, she'd never want for anything again, and she certainly wouldn't have to work. But she enjoyed working in the boutique. It gave her a sense of purpose and independence, although the idea of becoming a countess was appealing. On a couple of occasions recently, she'd found herself rolling the name around her head to see how it sounded.

Ruby Nightingale, the Countess of Ruttingham.

It had a nice ring to it and it gave her a fuzzy feeling whenever Hugo reserved tables at restaurants as the Viscount Ruttingham. The name opened doors and freed up tables. But the thought of being married to Hugo for the rest of her life filled her with dread. He wasn't exactly bad looking, but he was a crushing bore and was always onto her about how she wore her hair and the length of her skirts. Sometimes she wished she could just walk away and forget she'd ever met him at that party on the Kings Road when she'd had one too many Moscow Mules and spent the night dancing until she was fit to drop.

'So what are you going to do?' Yolanda asked.

'I'm not sure.' Ruby felt like the weight of the world was pressing down on her shoulders.

'Don't string him along too long. If he's not right for you, you shouldn't be wasting his time or yours.'

'I suppose you're right.' Ruby glanced over Yolanda's head and caught the time on the big clock on the wall. 'Is it okay if I take my lunch now?'

'Of course. Go.'

Ruby grabbed her sandwich and the novel she'd almost finished from her bag and, as it was a beautiful day with only a few wisps of cloud in the sky, headed for a quiet corner of Hyde Park.

As she walked, her mind remained on Hugo, wondering whether it was time to finally tell him how she was felt. But Hugo wasn't used to rejection. Whatever Hugo wanted, Hugo usually got. But if things weren't right between them, she shouldn't be pretending everything was fine. Yolanda was absolutely right. She'd have to speak to him. Raise the subject gently. Who knows, he might be feeling the same way, although she doubted it. He doted on her, always bringing her little gifts and flowers or taking her out to fancy restaurants. There was no doubt he'd take it hard if she tried to break it off. And was that what she really wanted, anyway? She'd never have the chance to become a countess again. It was a once in a lifetime opportunity. But if she didn't love him ...

The squeal of tyres and the furious blast of a horn as Ruby stepped onto a crossing snapped her back to the moment with a terrifying jolt. She saw a flash of green paint and barely had time to scream before the car was bearing down on her, the face behind the windscreen contorted in anguish.

And in the brief seconds before the car hit, everything froze in time. The glint of sunlight on the windscreen. The smell of diesel fumes from a passing bus. The warmth of the sun on her arms. The thud of her heart in her chest. And the sight of her novel falling from her hand with her sandwich, slices of bread, ham and tomato spilling across the asphalt.

Chapter 4

The man with the heavy-rimmed glasses who'd found me sleeping earlier stepped back, his eyes opening wide with alarm. 'Hey, easy,' he said, throwing up his arms defensively as clenched my fists, ready to take a swing at him. His wife was standing behind him with a couple of small bags and the two girls still preoccupied with their phones.

'What do you want?' I snapped. 'Were you following me?'

'We were worried about you, that's all. We saw you staggering around,' the man said.

'And if anything had happened, we'd never have forgiven ourselves,' his wife added.

'I wish you'd just leave me alone. I'm fine.'

'We'd feel better if you let someone look at your head,' the man said.

They were only trying to help, but really, I was perfectly alright. A little groggy, maybe, but I'm sure it wasn't anything serious. Finding Ruby was all I cared about. She was the one who needed help, not me.

'I can't,' I said. 'Not until I've found my wife. I think she's in trouble.'

'Trouble?' The woman stepped in front of her husband and rested a hand on my arm. 'What kind of trouble?'

'I don't know,' I said. 'I can't explain it. It's just a feeling.'

'Can you remember when you last saw her?'

My head drooped. 'No.'

The woman frowned. 'Were you supposed to be catching a flight?'

'No.' I shook my head. It was about the one thing I was certain of. 'We flew in last night from Rome. We were on our honeymoon.'

The woman raised a quizzical eyebrow.

'We were married last week,' I sighed. I don't know why I was bothering to tell them. I'm sure they didn't care. 'In Buckinghamshire, where her parents live.'

'Congratulations.'

'We'd spent the night at a club,' I explained. 'The last thing I remember is walking back to our hotel and Ruby dancing through a piazza. I can't remember anything at all after that.'

'Nothing?' the man asked.

'No.' I was sure it would all come back to me in time, but right now my mind was a blank.

'But you're certain you caught a flight home together last night?'

'We must have done.'

'She must be here somewhere,' the man's wife said, rubbing my arm. 'Don't worry, we'll find her.'

I wish I shared her confidence, but I couldn't help the gnawing feeling that Ruby wasn't lost. She was in trouble. Serious trouble. And she desperately needed my help. I couldn't explain why I felt so sure of it. Some kind of sixth sense. A gut feeling. And the longer she was missing, the stronger the feeling grew.

'What does she look like?' the man asked. 'We could keep an eye out for her, if you like?'

'I suppose,' I said. Anything to get them off my back. 'She's tall. Not quite as tall as me.' I held up my hand, palm flat, in front of my nose to give them an approximation of her height. 'And she has long, blonde hair, the colour of wheat right before an autumn harvest. And slate grey eyes and the biggest smile you've ever seen. You'll know her if you see her. She's the most beautiful woman in the world,' I said, with a lump balling in my throat.

The woman smiled. 'She's obviously a very special lady.' I know she meant well, but the way she said it came across as patronising.

'Any idea what she might have been wearing?' the man asked.

'I don't know.' The tears I'd been fighting pooled in my eyes. 'I don't remember anything.'

'It's okay,' the woman soothed. 'Don't upset yourself. We'll find her.'

I wiped my eyes with the side of my finger and sniffed, ashamed of my tears. I pulled my shoulders back, composing myself. 'I thought you had a flight to catch?'

'Delayed.' The man checked his watch. 'We have time to kill.'

'Which means we can help you find your wife,' the woman added with a sweet smile.

'Her name's Ruby,' I said, reminding them she had a name.

'Of course. We'll help you find Ruby. Why don't we sit down for a moment and see if there's anything you can remember about the flight.' The woman tried to coax me away from the wall, back to the seating area where they'd first found me.

I found my resistance weakening. After all, I had no one else. Without Ruby, I was on my own. I let the woman lead me through the river of people still streaming along the corridor to a row of empty seats where I sat, my mind turning over and over, trying to remember something, anything, about the last twenty-four hours, after Ruby and I had returned to the Regis Hotel.

I tried picturing the airport in Rome. The check-in desks. The departure lounge. The aircraft. The punch of the seat in my back as we took off. Ruby, her eyes screwed tightly shut, gripping my hand for reassurance as she had when we'd left for Italy. But it was all a blank. Why couldn't I recall any of it? It had to be in my head somewhere. It was just a matter of accessing it. At least if I could remember what Ruby was wearing, that might help. But I couldn't. There was nothing. Only a big, black hole where my memories should have been.

I thumped a fist on my thigh in frustration, angry with myself.

'Hey,' the woman said, snatching my wrist. 'Don't beat yourself up. We're going to find her.

Everything is going to be alright, okay?'

But I had a horrible feeling that everything would not be alright. It was like I was standing on the precipice of a cliff, waiting for news that would send me plummeting over the edge.

'Look,' the man said, pointing at the concourse below.

Two police officers were clutching ugly-looking semi-automatic rifles to their chests, their rubber-soled black boots squeaking across the tiled floor. They were chatting casually while their eyes scanned left and right, vigilantly sweeping for threats.

'I'll speak to them,' the man said. 'They'll know what to do.'

And before I could stop him, he was hurrying for a set of concrete stairs that wound down to the floor below.

'I don't want the police involved,' I shouted after him.

But he was gone without a backwards glance.

'Whyever not?' the woman asked.

I couldn't explain why, but just as I was sure Ruby was in trouble, I had the distinct sense that I couldn't trust the police, that maybe even they had something to do with her disappearance.

'I - I ...' I stammered.

The woman stared at me, waiting for me to answer.

I turned my head to watch as her husband emerged onto the concourse and strode purposefully towards the two officers. He stopped them with a raised hand and waved his arms animatedly as he talked to them. Then pointed up towards us. When they looked up and saw me, my blood ran cold. My heart thudded, and I knew I couldn't let them catch me. That I had to run.

'I have to go,' I said, jumping up.

'What? Where?' the woman sprang back, surprised by my burst of energy.

'No police,' I gasped. 'I'm sorry.'

'But -'

I glanced back a final time. The officers were on the move, following the man towards the stairs. Coming for me. Three serious faces. I shuddered with fear. If they caught me, I wouldn't be able to help Ruby.

I took refuge in the throng of people trampling along the walkway, clutching coffees and bags and children and phones. I weaved between them following a zig-zagging path, bumping and jostling as I went, drawing tuts and rolled eyes. Past the newsagent. And the currency exchange bureau. When I reached the cafe where the queue for coffee had grown even longer, I chanced a quick look back.

At first I couldn't see them. I ducked behind a wall that separated a seating area in the cafe from the corridor and peered back the way I'd come. A sea of bobbing heads, but no police. I held my breath, praying I'd given them the slip, and they'd given up.

But just as I relaxed, they appeared, parting waves of travellers as they marched towards me. They both looked so young. Ruddy-cheeked and dark-haired. Slightly menacing in their black uniforms, their trousers tucked into the tops of their boots and body armour plumping out their chests. Rifles cocked. Eyes roaming. I had the distinct impression I was being hunted. Had they been looking for me even before the man had approached them? In which case, his tipoff had been a fortuitous stroke of luck for them and incredibly unlucky for me. What were the chances?

I had to move, otherwise they were going to find me. The one advantage I had was the crowds of people. If I could blend in, there was a possibility I could disappear among them, but time wasn't on my side. The officers were closing in with every step.

With my nerves jangling, I turned to hurry away, my head down and my shoulders hunched. But as I pirouetted, not looking where I was going, I tripped, clattering into a cleaner's cart I'd not seen parked behind me. I fell sprawling across the floor, sending two mops flying. I landed awkwardly on my side and grimaced as a bolt of pain jarred through my knee.

A cleaner in a high visibility jacket stared down at me in horror.

'Hey Sir, I'm so sorry. Are you okay? Did you hurt yourself?' he asked in a thick Eastern European accent.

'I hurt my knee,' I said, trying to sit up.

He grabbed me under my arm and lifted me slowly to my feet. I saw his gaze drift towards the cut on my head and the fear slide across his face.

'No, no, it's okay,' I said, touching the skin around the wound with the tips of my fingers. 'I did this earlier.'

'I thought you'd seen the cart,' he said, looking me up and down. 'Sorry, sorry, sorry.'

'It's okay.' I rubbed my knee. 'It's not your fault.'

'Please, I beg you not to report it. I could lose job.'

The two police officers were terrifyingly close, marching unrelentingly towards me. The cleaner followed my gaze. 'Are they looking for you?' he asked.

I thought about lying, but what was the point?

I fixed him with a steely gaze. 'Yes,' I said. 'Will you help me?'

He took a step back, his eyes narrowing. I know what it must have looked like. Nobody runs from the police unless they're guilty of something.

'Please,' I begged.

Chapter 5

The man shrugged off his high visibility vest. 'Put this on,' he said. 'Quickly.'

I didn't wait to be told twice. I yanked it on over my shirt. Then he gave me his baseball cap which I pulled down low over my eyes as he picked up the mops I'd knocked over and stood them in a bucket on the end of the cart, releasing a waft of bleach fumes which clawed the back of my throat.

'Take this,' he said, manoeuvring the cart in front of me. 'Keep your head down and follow me. Hurry.'

To my surprise, he headed directly towards the two police officers who were now so close I could see the dark shadow of their stubble and the acne on the chin of the younger one. I lowered my gaze under the peak of my cap and followed close on the cleaner's heels, holding my breath.

We passed the officers barely a few metres away, but they didn't break stride, the high visibility jacket I'd donned ironically rendering me virtually invisible. I couldn't stop a smile curling across my lips.

We turned down the side of the currency exchange bureau, where a door was concealed in the wall. The cleaner punched a code into a keypad, and the door swung open to reveal a large store cupboard. He took the cart from me and pushed it inside as a light flickered on.

'I'm not supposed to let anyone in here,' he said, pushing the cart under a shelf laden with plastic bottles of cleaning fluid, cans of polish, rolls of paper towels, buckets and multi-coloured cloths. 'Please, not tell anyone, okay?'

I wriggled out of the high visibility vest, scrunched it up, and handed it back with the cap. 'I won't. Thank you.'

'You like tea?'

I nodded.

He filled a kettle at a stainless steel sink and set it to boil on a chipboard shelf where a row of mugs were lined up alongside a glass container filled with teabags.

I pulled up a plastic chair and sat down, my legs trembling. I just needed a moment to gather my thoughts.

'My name is Stan,' the cleaner said, dropping teabags into two mugs as the kettle hissed and gurgled.

'Victor.'

'How is your knee?'

'It's fine,' I said. I'd almost forgotten I'd hurt myself. I gave it an absentminded rub through my trousers.

'You won't report it?'

'What?'

'I could lose job,' he said, staring at me earnestly.

'No,' I said. 'I wasn't looking where I was going.'

'Thank you.'

'You're welcome, but I should be thanking you,' I said. 'I don't know what you must think about me, trying to avoid the police like that.' I laughed nervously.

Stan shrugged like he'd seen it all before, and worse. 'What you do to your head?' He was tall and skinny as if his metabolism burned off food faster than he could eat.

'I can't remember,' I said. 'I guess I must have fallen and banged it.'

'Maybe you need to see doctor?'

'Maybe,' I said. 'But not right now. I'm looking for my wife. We flew home from our honeymoon in Italy last night, but now she's missing and I can't remember anything about the flight home or arriving back at the airport. It's all a blank.' I don't know why I had the sudden urge to tell him everything.

'Because of your head?' He touched his own temple with the tips of his fingers. 'You should definitely see doctor.'

'I can't. Not until I've found Ruby.'

'So why hiding from police?' Stan asked, his brow furrowing. 'They can help find her, no?'

I squeezed the bridge of my nose, running my thumb and forefinger over my eyes. 'No, I don't trust them.'

'Why not?'

'Something happened after we landed and now they're looking for me. I'm worried the police might have something to do with her disappearance.'

Stan frowned. God knows what he was thinking.

'Was she ...' He glanced at his feet.

'What?'

'Drugs?'

'What? No! Of course not. It's nothing like that. She's done nothing wrong,' I said. 'Whatever it is, they've made a mistake. I just need to work out what's going on.'

Stan sloshed boiling water into the mugs, added a splash of milk and hooked out the teabags with a spoon. 'Here,' he said.

'Thank you. I mean, for helping me. You didn't need to do that.'

'No problem. You stay here for little while, but my supervisor, he'll be looking for me soon. You must leave. Understand?'

'It's okay. You've been really kind.'

'I hope you find your wife,' Stan said.

'I will. I'm not leaving here without her.'

He sat on a chair by the sink and sipped his tea. 'Tell me about your wedding.'

I cast my mind back. Every little detail was indelibly fixed in my mind. 'It was amazing,' I said. 'The best day of my life, although it already feels like a lifetime ago.' A lump swelled in my throat as I remembered Ruby arriving at the church in a simple white silk dress inlaid with lace and pearl, the most beautiful bride I'd ever seen. I'd felt like the luckiest man alive. 'Are you married, Stan?'

'Married, yes. Two children. A boy and a girl, seven and eight.'

I nodded. I doubted a job cleaning at the airport paid much to keep a family of four fed and clothed.

'What's your wife's name?'

'Serena.' He smiled when he said her name, but it quickly evaporated, his face creasing into a frown. 'Maybe you ask at help desk about Ruby,' he said. 'They might have information.'

'I wish it was that simple.'

'Maybe she got lost in airport. It's big place. What flight were you on?'

'I don't know. It was a flight from Rome. That's all I can remember.'

'But your ticket? You can check,' he said, his eyes opening wide.

'Yes, of course, you're right! My ticket. I don't know why I didn't think of that.' I jumped up, sloshing tea over the floor, and patted my pockets, looking for my wallet.

But all I could find was my handkerchief and a half-eaten packet of mints. I was missing my jacket too. I'm sure I would have been wearing one. I always wore a jacket. I felt underdressed without one.

'What's wrong?' Stan asked.

'My wallet. It's gone.'

'Are you sure?'

'Yes, I'm sure,' I snapped. 'Someone must have robbed me while I was sleeping.' As if my day couldn't get any worse. Now what the hell was I going to do?

Stan blinked at me.

Shit. My passport. It should have been in my jacket pocket with my wallet. That was missing too, along with our luggage.

Someone had cleaned us out and taken everything. And now I had nothing. No money. No passport. No bags. And worst of all, no Ruby. I dropped my head in my hands.

'I think you need to speak to police,' Stan said.

'No, I can't,' I said, shaking my head resolutely. 'I told you, I don't trust them.'

'Then what you going to do?'

I looked up at Stan, feeling hopelessly lost and alone. I needed help, but I couldn't go to the police, at least not until I'd worked out what had happened to Ruby and why they were looking for me.

'I have absolutely no idea,' I said.

Chapter 6

As Ruby lay winded in the road, staring up at the sky with a dull ache in her shoulder and the top of her leg, she considered herself lucky not to have been killed. The sports car, travelling too fast, had clipped her hip and sent her flying off her feet and sprawling across the floor. She tried to sit up, gathering her skirt around her legs, mindful of her modesty as a figure loomed over her, blocking out the sun.

'Good God, are you hurt?' the man asked as he helped her back onto her feet. 'You stepped out right in front of me. There was nothing I could do.'

'You were travelling far too fast.' Ruby brushed herself down and glanced ruefully at what was left of her sandwich scattered across the road, slices of buttered bread, tomato and ham caked in grit and dirt.

'You didn't look,' the man said. 'You just walked into the road.'

The man's car had come to a halt sideways, its engine still idling.

'You could have killed me,' she said.

'Well, yes, I'm sorry about that.' He stood back and looked her up and down, then picked up her novel and handed it to her. 'But no harm done, although I'm afraid your lunch is probably ruined.'

'Is that your professional assessment?' Ruby trembled. Suddenly, she didn't feel too good. Her legs were weak and her throat was dry. 'I think I might need to sit down for a bit,' she said.

'Probably just the shock.' The man escorted her to the pavement and sat her on a bench while he waved away a concerned crowd of onlookers who had gathered ashen-faced to see what all the fuss was about.

'Nothing to see here,' the man said, shooing everyone away. 'Thank you for your concern. The lady's fine.'

'Someone ought to call the police,' a gruff male voice said.

'Does she need an ambulance?' a woman asked.

'No, no, everything's under control, thank you. No need to call anyone.'

The man jumped in his car and manoeuvred it to the side of the road. After a few minutes, buses and taxis began hurtling past again and the bustle and buzz of the busy London street resumed as if nothing had happened.

'Are you quite sure you're okay?' the man asked, sitting with her on the bench. 'It must have been a bit of a shock.'

Ruby rolled her shoulder and winced. 'Yes, I'll be okay.'

'Let me make it up to you. Can I take you for lunch? It's the least I can do. I know a lovely little bistro around the corner. I'm sure they'd find us a table.'

'Really, there's no need. Thank you,' Ruby said.

'Please, I insist.'

A wide smile lit up his face. He was broad-shouldered and wide-chested, and easily six feet tall, if not more, with a disarming charm and an affable confidence. So different to Hugo with his weaselly arrogance and sense of entitlement. Ruby subtly checked his hand for a wedding ring and when she saw there was none, accepted his offer. She might as well get lunch out of him after he'd nearly killed her.

'Wonderful.' He jumped up with the energy of a gazelle. 'The name's Victor Cano, by the way.'

'Ruby Aubrey.'

'That's a bit of a tongue twister,' he said, making her blush as he took her hand and kissed it like he was a medieval knight courting a virginal maiden. 'Pleased to meet you, Ruby Aubrey.'

They drove to an intimate little restaurant off the Cromwell Road and sat at a table for two where they ate meatballs and Victor ordered a bottle of expensive red wine, even though it was only lunchtime.

To her surprise, Ruby found Victor was most personable company, listening to her answers attentively as he quizzed her about her job at Yolanda's boutique and her work at the women's refuge. In return, he told her he was the director of a property development company and that he liked fast cars and horse racing. She discovered they both liked to read, and he surprised her again with his knowledge of Harper Lee and Sylvia Plath, although he said he preferred Le Carré, MacLean and Fleming.

Their conversation flowed so freely that when Ruby checked her watch, she was shocked to see she was going to be late getting back to work.

'I'm so sorry, I have to go,' she said, folding up her napkin and laying it on the table. 'I'm supposed to be back at work by two. Yolanda will be getting worried.'

'Don't worry, I'll drive you,' Victor said, catching the waiter's attention for the bill.

'It's alright, I can walk,' Ruby said. 'It's not far.'

'Nonsense. You're already late. My fault again.'

'Well, if you're sure?'

'I'm more than sure. I insist.'

Victor pulled out a wad of notes from his pocket to pay and made a point of thanking the staff for their attentiveness - something Hugo would never have done. Then he dropped her off directly outside the boutique. Yolanda was sure to have seen. She never missed a trick. But Ruby didn't care, even though she knew she'd have to face a barrage of questions from her boss.

'Can I see you again?' Victor asked, running around the front of the car to open Ruby's door like a true gent.

'Oh, I don't know,' Ruby said, flustered, and with only a fleeting thought to what she would say to Hugo. 'I suppose so.'

She scribbled her number on a scrap of paper and trotted into the shop, glowing as Victor pulled away in a squeal of tyres and a throaty roar from the car's engine.

Yolanda's mouth was gaping open when Ruby walked in. It was too much to hope that she'd not seen Victor dropping her off in his fancy sports car. 'Ruby Aubrey,' she said, sounding outraged. 'Who was that man?'

'I'm sorry I'm late.' Ruby dropped her book in her bag behind the counter.

'Never mind that. Who was he? Tell me everything.'

'Oh, him?' Ruby said, glancing casually out of the window. 'I think that might be the man I'm going to marry.'

She'd only said it to see how Yolanda would react, but as the words tripped off her tongue, it suddenly didn't seem such an outlandish idea. There was an undeniable chemistry between them. Victor was handsome, well dressed, obviously had a good job and money, but more importantly, he liked her. A lot. Why else would he ask for her number?

The only problem was Hugo.

But she didn't care. All she could think about was the way her stomach had fizzed when their hands had accidentally touched in the restaurant and now she couldn't shake Victor Cano from her thoughts. She made her mind up. No matter what happened between her and Victor, there was no place in her life for Hugo. Daddy would be cross, of course, but what was the point of wasting your time with a man who didn't make you feel special? Why squander a lifetime with a man you didn't love?

'What are you going to tell Hugo?' Yolanda asked.

'I don't know,' Ruby said with a smile. She was still buzzing. 'I'll figure something out, I'm sure.'

Chapter 7

Stan dropped my empty mug in the sink and tugged on his high visibility vest. 'I must get back to work. I'm sorry,' he said.

I stood and pushed the chair back into the corner where I'd found it.

'I understand. Thank you for your kindness.'

'What will you do now?'

'I need to keep looking for Ruby and find my wallet and jacket,' I said. 'Otherwise I'm stuck here.'

There were only two realistic options to explain Ruby's disappearance. Either she'd been detained after we'd landed or we'd been separated at a later stage, although neither scenario made much sense.

If customs or immigration had stopped Ruby as we'd come off the plane, why hadn't I stayed with her? I wouldn't have abandoned her. But if we had made it through unimpeded, why had I stayed the night at the airport? Was it because I'd already lost Ruby? Or because I'd lost my wallet? And what about the injury to my head? Had we been mugged and our money, passport and luggage stolen? It was possible, I supposed, but it didn't bring me any closer to understanding why Ruby was missing.

I shook Stan's hand. He had a firm, reassuring grip. 'Thank you for your kindness,' I said again. 'I owe you a drink when I've found my wallet.'

'No problem. I hope you find your wife.'

As I cracked open the door to leave, an automated message echoed around the airport. I'd heard it played before between announcements about delayed flights and details of departure gates, but I'd not paid much attention to it. It warned travellers to be vigilant for any suspicious bags left unattended. It gave me an idea.

'Is there an information desk near here?' I asked Stan.

'Downstairs in arrivals hall,' he said, pulling out his cart and filling up a bucket with clean water.

'Brilliant, thank you.'

A steady stream of people was still flowing long the walkway outside the storeroom, mostly heading for the departure lounge, but I couldn't see the police patrol. Hopefully, they'd moved onto another part of the airport. I hunched my shoulders and crammed my hands in my pockets, trying to make myself as invisible as I'd been when I'd followed Stan with the cleaning cart.

I reached the flight of stairs close to where I'd been asleep and made my way down to the concourse below. The information desk was squeezed between a high street pharmacy and an airport concierge service. A woman with short, blonde hair and a tattoo of a butterfly on her wrist was sitting behind a bank of computer screens tapping at a keyboard. With a deep breath, I approached the counter.

The woman looked up and smiled. 'Can I help?'

'I've lost my wife,' I said.

'I'm sorry to hear that, Sir.'

'I was wondering if you could put out an announcement over the public address system?'

She grabbed a pad of paper and a pen. 'Of course. What's her name?'

'Ruby,' I said. 'Ruby Cano. We're newlyweds. Just back from our honeymoon.' I thought that might make her more sympathetic to my request.

The woman scribbled down Ruby's name as I spelt it out. 'Right, okay. And where did you last see her?'

I could hardly tell her my last memory of Ruby was of us together in Italy. She would think I was mad. 'We were on a flight from Rome that landed last night.'

'Last night?' She frowned, her pen in mid-air.

'We fell asleep in one of the waiting areas upstairs and when I woke this morning, she'd gone,' I said, realising how totally ridiculous it all sounded.

'What have you done to your head?'

'It's nothing. A scratch,' I said. 'Can you put out an announcement or not?'

'Of course. Don't you worry. We'll find her. Now, what was the flight number?'

So many bloody questions. Why couldn't she just make the announcement? 'Why do you need to know that?'

Her smile slipped. 'There's no need to take that tone,' she said.

'I've forgotten the flight number.'

'Okay, it doesn't matter. Hang on here and I'll put a call out for her.'

I stepped away from the counter as a man in a beige linen suit approached, dragging an enormous case on wheels behind him. The woman held a finger up to him as she hunched over a microphone on a long stalk. Her voice echoed around the airport through dozens of unseen speakers.

'This is an announcement for passenger Ruby Cano on a flight from Rome. Please make your way to the information desk in the arrivals hall at your earliest convenience. That's passenger Ruby Cano to the information desk.'

I smiled my appreciation at the woman and edged away to stand in a corner between the desk and the concierge bureau, not sure what to do, other than to stand and wait, praying Ruby had heard the announcement and was on her way back to me. I imagined her battling through the crowds with a sheepish look on her face, but I didn't hold my breath. I didn't believe for one second she had simply walked away from me and become lost. My gut was still telling me she was in serious trouble. But where?

A minute passed. And then two.

A man walked past with a screaming toddler in the midst of a full-on tantrum. He stopped right in front of me and smacked her smartly across the back of the legs, stunning the child into a temporary silence. Then he crouched down to her height so their noses were almost touching, gripped her arms tightly, and yelled in her face.

'If you don't stop crying, I'll give you something to properly cry about, and then I'll take you home and you can stay with Granny,' he screamed. 'And you can forget about coming on holiday with us.'

The kid snivelled and wiped a hand across her nose, her eyes wet and bloodshot.

I felt sick to the pit of my stomach. It reminded me of how my father could lose his temper in a flash, the slightest transgression causing him to erupt with unbridled fury and violence. Until my mother finally saw sense and divorced him. Thankfully, I hadn't seen him since I was ten.

After waiting five minutes, the woman at the information desk leaned over the counter and waved at me.

'Any sign of her?' she asked.

I shook my head.

'What about trying the airline?' she said. 'They might have some information.'

'I don't know how to -'

'Which airline was it? I can call them, if you like.'

I cast my mind back, but even that memory was fuzzy. 'British Airways,' I said, guessing. I always flew British Airways.

The woman smiled sympathetically. 'Give me two minutes,' she said, picking up a phone and dialling a number.

I stepped away to keep watching the people streaming through the concourse. If Ruby appeared, I didn't want to miss her.

'Mr Cano?' The woman beckoned me over after a few minutes, worry lines furrowing her brow.

'Yes?'

'Are you absolutely certain you flew in last night? You couldn't have been mistaken?' she said.

'It was last night,' I said firmly. 'I only wish I could remember the flight number.'

'Okay, well I've spoken to the British Airways team, but I'm afraid they're a bit confused.'

'What do you mean, confused?'

'They've checked the manifests of all their flights from Rome yesterday,' the woman said, 'and no one with the name Ruby Cano was on any of them.'

Chapter 8

Ruby swore there was a tear in her father's eye when he first saw her on the morning of her wedding.

'Ruby,' he gasped, as she tip-toed down the stairs, trying not to trip in the figure-hugging silky ivory dress that made her look like a princess. 'You look beautiful.'

He took his daughter's hand and kissed her cheek as her mother fussed with her train and her bridesmaids giggled and jostled with excitement.

'Do I look okay?'

'You look like a million dollars. Victor's a very lucky man. Now hurry, your carriage awaits.'

He threw open the front door to reveal a splendid vintage Rolls Royce parked on the gravel drive, so sparkly clean you could see your face in the paintwork.

He helped Ruby climb onto the back seat and sat with her hand in his lap as they pulled away from the house for the short journey to the church. It was so close they could have walked, as they did on frosty mornings every Christmas Day. But not today. Her father insisted they drive through the village where so many people had come out to wave and cheer. She felt like royalty.

'You might be getting married, but you know I'll always be here for you, don't you?' he said, as the car rolled through the church gates. 'No matter what happens.'

'Stop it, you'll make me cry. I can't walk into church with mascara running down my face.'

'I mean it,' he said, squeezing her hand. 'You'll always be my little girl.'

That was it. She knew he'd set her off. 'Quick, do you have a tissue?' she murmured, as tears welled in her eyes.

He pulled a fresh white handkerchief from his pocket. 'Here, use this.'

She dabbed the tears, careful not to smudge her make-up as the Rolls Royce came to a gentle halt outside the church.

Her father had been remarkably understanding when she'd told him she'd broken up with Hugo, at least outwardly. It was no secret that he'd been hoping Hugo would propose and that Ruby would be elevated into the nobility, but when he saw how happy Victor made her, he couldn't be cross. And when Victor asked Ruby to marry him nine months after he'd nearly killed her, her father happily gave his blessing.

An organ heralded Ruby's arrival with a reedy blast. The church fell silent and a hundred heads turned to watch as Ruby grabbed her father's arm and he walked her down the aisle.

Victor looked so dapper in his grey suit, a soppy smile plastered across his freshly-shaven face, ruddy cheeks glowing, his eyes sparkling. Ruby was the happiest woman alive.

'Do you take this man to be your lawfully wedded husband?' the vicar asked.

I do. I do. I absolutely do.

She'd never been more sure of anything.

The ceremony went without a hitch, apart from a nervous stumble over her vows and one of the young bridesmaids singing to herself during the prayers, much to the muted amusement of their guests. But Ruby didn't mind. Having children at the service made it feel like a proper family occasion.

Ruby and Victor had talked about having children and both agreed they'd like a large family. She pictured a house full of children, with fun and laughter filling every room. She couldn't wait to get started. The day she met Victor was like the beginning of a new book and their wedding the start of a new chapter. They were going to spend the rest of their lives together, raising children, growing old, and nurturing grandchildren. Who could want any more than that?

They held a lavish reception in a marquee in the grounds of Ruby's parents' house, where champagne corks popped and they gorged on a feast prepared by a French chef Ruby's father had flown in from Provence. It was perfect. And as the sun set and a full moon reared its head in a star-speckled sky, the band took their places on stage and Victor and Ruby shared their first dance.

Victor placed his hands on Ruby's hips and stared into her eyes so intently she thought she would melt.

'I love you, Mrs Cano,' he said.

'And I love you, Mr Cano.'

When their lips met in a lingering kiss that flipped Ruby's stomach upside down, everyone clapped and cheered. She blushed and hid her head in Victor's shoulder, but her embarrassment was short-lived as everyone poured onto the dance floor with their partners and the band struck up a more lively tune. Soon the whole tent was swinging.

'I need a glass of water,' Ruby whispered in Victor's ear as she pulled away from him, heading for the bar.

'Don't be long,' he said, with a wink, before turning and grabbing her mother and twirling her around in time to the music.

Ruby giggled as she walked away, wishing she could pause the moment so she could remember it for all eternity. The day had flashed past at triple speed and soon it would be over. At least they had Rome to look forward to. They were due to fly at eleven the next day and had the entire week to themselves. Her father had even arranged for them to stay in a smart hotel in the centre of the city.

The barman handed Ruby a glass with a kindly smile, but as she headed back to her table to rest her weary feet, there was a commotion on the dance floor. Men jostling. Women edging away. Raised voices. Pushing and shoving.

And suddenly, as the throng parted, Hugo staggered into view, so drunk he could hardly stand up straight. Victor snatched him by the shoulder and spun him around. Hugo took a pathetic swipe at him with his fist, which Victor easily swatted away.

What on earth was he doing here trying to ruin her day?

Ruby ran to the dance floor and pushed Victor to one side. She couldn't allow him to get into a fight on their wedding. There was no way she'd allow that to be the enduring image of the day.

'Hugo, what are you doing here?' she hissed.

His eyes were glassy and black, his hair ruffled. He swayed from side to side as he tried to focus on her face.

'Ruby!' he said, a sickly smile creeping across his lips. 'You look absolutely ravishing.'

'You shouldn't be here,' she said, taking his arm and guiding him off the dance floor, nodding to the band to carry on playing.

'But I love you,' he slurred. 'You've made a terrible mistake, but it's not too late for us.'

'What? Are you insane?' she said, as they stepped out of the bright lights in the marquee and into the gloom of the garden, out of sight and earshot of their poor guests.

'Come on, Ruby, I know you feel the same.'

'How did you even get in here?'

He shrugged. 'There was nobody to stop me.'

'I don't want you here.'

'You don't mean that,' he said, a sadness in his eyes.

'Hugo, I don't love you. I love Victor. He's my husband. Now you're making a fool of yourself. Please, just go.'

Ruby sensed a figure appear behind her. She thought it was Victor but was pleased to see it was her father, a reassuring presence in a difficult predicament.

'What's going on Hugo?' he demanded.

'Sir Nigel.' Hugo's Adam's apple bobbed up and down. 'I came to tell Ruby I still love her.'

'On her wedding day?' Her father scowled. 'Are you totally out of your mind?'

'I think she's made a terrible mistake. Who is he anyway, this husband of hers? Some common businessman, I heard. Think what I can offer her.'

'It's time you left.' Her father grabbed Hugo's arm roughly.

Hugo snatched it back, staggering to catch his balance. 'I'm not going anywhere,' he shouted. 'Not until Ruby comes to her senses.'

Out of the shadows, three men in black suits and dark ties appeared. If they'd been at the reception earlier, Ruby hadn't noticed them. But then there were so many people her father had invited she didn't know. There were at least three MPs and countless grey men with thinning hair and looping moustaches she didn't recognise. Important people her father knew through his job. She wasn't sure exactly what he did at MI5 because it was all very secret and she wasn't supposed to ask, but it was a senior position and he had lots of influential contacts.

With a slight nod from her father, the three men pounced on Hugo and dragged him away. He fought and spat and yelled but was quickly overpowered and removed from the garden with minimal fuss, like an unwelcome spider plucked out of the shower and tossed out of the bathroom window.

'What are they going to do to him?' Ruby asked, as her father placed a warm hand on her shoulder and led her back inside.

'Don't worry about that,' he said.

'Are they going to hurt him?'

'All you need to know is that you'll never be bothered by Hugo Nightingale again,' he said.

Chapter 9

I staggered backwards with the sensation the floor was falling away from under my feet, my head swimming with confusion.

'B - but that's impossible,' I stammered.

The blonde woman on the information desk shrugged. 'It could be a computer glitch,' she said. 'I'm sorry.'

It had to be an error. Of course Ruby had been on the flight home with me. Where else could she be? I wouldn't have flown home without her. My heart thrashed in my tightening chest.

'Sir, are you okay?' the woman asked, her voice sounding hollow.

'I'm fine,' I puffed, edging away.

'Is there anything else I can help you with?'

But I'd already turned away, stumbling across the concourse like a drunken bum, struggling to make sense out of why there wan no record of Ruby on any flights from Rome.

Could that be the reason she'd been arrested when we'd landed? Had she somehow sneaked onto the plane and been caught when we arrived?

It would explain why she wasn't on the manifest. But how would that even be possible? It was absurd, but I couldn't think of any other explanation to fit the facts. Perhaps we'd both been stowaways and somehow I'd made it through alone without being detected. It would at least explain why the police were looking for me.

But we'd had return tickets booked, and there hadn't been a problem on the flight out. I could remember that clearly enough. Ruby had a seat by the window over the wing and I'd sat in the middle between her and an Italian businessman in a sharp blue suit. I even remembered delighting in making a fearsome-looking border control officer at the airport in Rome crack a smile when I mentioned we were visiting on our honeymoon. So if there hadn't been an issue getting into Rome, what had happened on the way home that had caused us such problems?

I needed to think.

And to work out what to do next.

Once again, I battled against the tide of weary travellers as a flight as more returning passengers poured into the arrivals hall. I stepped out of the way to let the surge die down, and hovered near a pillar, watching people emerge in small groups with trolleys of luggage through four staggered glass security tunnels. Each glass tunnel had automatic doors at either end that acted as a secure one-way passage out into the hall under a prominent sign warning against unauthorised access into what was a restricted area.

If Ruby was being held in the secure inner confines of the airport, this could be my way of reaching her. Without a ticket or passport, I couldn't see any other option.

I studied the glass tunnels carefully and noticed what looked to be a flaw in their design. At times, doors at both ends of the tunnels were open simultaneously as one passenger entered and another exited. If you timed it just right, and ran quickly, you could make it through in the opposite direction without being detected. It would be an enormous risk, but to save Ruby, it was one I had to take. It had only been a week since we'd exchanged vows. To have and to hold, for better or for worse. That was my role now as her husband. I had a duty to protect her, no matter what it took.

I glanced back towards the information desk on the off-chance Ruby had miraculously heard the announcement and had made her way there to find me. There was a snaking queue of people waiting for attention, but no sign of my wife there or anywhere else in the concourse. I let my eyes skip from one face to another in the sea of people, scrutinising hundreds, thousands of strangers, and spotted the two police officers I'd slipped away from earlier. They were back down on the lower level, giving the impression they were strolling casually on patrol, looking relaxed as they chatted, but their eyes never stopped roving. Hunters' eyes. Patiently stalking their quarry. Time to move.

I scurried towards the stairs that headed up to the departure lounge and the seating area where I'd fallen asleep overnight. It was somewhere to regroup and think. I raced up the first half-a-dozen steps but then lost my footing and slipped. My body jolted forwards and then I was toppling back down, rolling and tumbling, all arms and legs as I tried to arrest my fall.

I came to a halt with the wind knocked out of my lungs and a sharp pain in my elbow and knee, although my pride was more damaged than my body as everyone stopped to stare. I prayed the commotion hadn't attracted the attention of the police.

A hand grabbed my arm, helping me up. I flinched at the touch, paranoia clouding my mind.

'That looked a nasty fall. Are you okay?'

I looked up into a woman's green eyes, her tangled hair spilling over her face.

'I slipped. I'm fine,' I said, dismissively.

'Nothing broken?'

'I don't think so.' I rubbed at a sharp spike of pain in my elbow.

With a loud drumming in my chest, I looked across the concourse to where I'd seen the police officers approaching.

'Oh dear, you've cut your head,' the woman said.

'What? No, I did that earlier,' I said, remembering the mystery wound on my temple. She must have thought I was totally accident prone.

The police had vanished. Maybe they'd detoured into a shop or had to respond to a call.

My shoulders slumped with relief.

'Are you flying somewhere or meeting someone?' the woman asked.

She was carrying a baby in a sling across her chest and gripping a bored-looking toddler by the hand.

'Err ... neither,' I said. 'I've lost my wife.'

She frowned.

'We flew in last night but got separated and now someone's stolen my jacket and wallet and all our bags.' At least I think that was true, the words cascading out of my mouth before I could stop them. 'I'm afraid my memory's a bit hazy.'

'Have you had breakfast? If you've lost your wallet, why don't you let me buy you something to eat,' she said.

'Really, there's no need,' I tried to protest. I couldn't even begin to think about food.

'At least let me buy you a coffee,' she said as the toddler began tugging her arm, trying to pull her away. 'If nothing else, I could do with the adult company.'

I really didn't want to be with anyone while I tried to figure out what had happened to Ruby, but the woman had been so kind to stop and help me to my feet. She was even offering to buy me breakfast.

'Sure,' I said, my resistance weakening. 'Why not?'

She grinned. 'Are you okay getting up the steps?'

God, she really did think I was a klutz.

'Yes, I'm fine,' I said, wincing as I took the first step and my knee protested.

The woman slipped a hand under my arm and took some of the weight off my leg, making me feel like an invalid.

'What about you?' I asked as I hobbled up the stairs. 'Are you catching a flight?'

'No, I'm waiting for my parents. They're due in from Majorca this morning. So how did you lose your wife?'

I shrugged. 'I don't know. We were on honeymoon in Rome -'

'Congratulations.'

'But I don't know what happened after that.'

We found a seat at a table in a cafe. The woman dropped a colourful woven bag off her shoulder and settled the toddler on a seat, snatching a teaspoon away from him as he tried to use it as a drumstick.

'I don't remember anything after our last night,' I explained. 'We went out for a meal and then found a club. I can remember Ruby - that's my wife - was so happy that night. She wouldn't stop dancing even on the way back to our hotel. But that's it. I can't remember anything after that.'

'How strange.'

'My mind is a complete blank. The next thing I remember is waking up in the airport, missing my wallet, my passport and our bags. Everything was gone. And no sign of Ruby anywhere.'

'Have you reported it?'

'Yes,' I lied. 'The police are looking into it.'

'Right.' She nodded, but the way she narrowed her eyes suggested she didn't believe me. 'Coffee?'

'Black. No sugar. Thank you. I'd offer to pay but ...'

'It's fine. I won't be a moment. Can you keep an eye on Charlie for me?'

I glanced at the little boy. I didn't have the first clue about kids, but I could hardly say no. But what if he started crying? Or tried to run off? Or made a scene? What was I supposed to do then? I couldn't believe this woman who I'd only just met was trusting me to look after her child.

'Of course,' I said, forcing a smile.

The little boy stared at me, a finger wedged up his nose. His mother smacked his hand down. 'Charlie, don't pick your nose. And be good for Mr...' She looked at me with raised eyebrows.

'Cano,' I said. 'Victor Cano.'

'Right, so be good for Mr Cano, and don't cause him any trouble.'

At that moment, the baby in her sling started thrashing and grizzling. She tried to soothe it, rocking her knees and swinging from side to side.

'Sorry, I think she needs her nappy changed. Are you okay here if I just pop to the ladies? Charlie, be good.'

She didn't wait for my answer. She just hurried off without a backwards glance, leaving Charlie and me staring at each other, neither of us sure what to say or do.

Chapter 10

Ruby threw open the door and gasped. 'Oh my God, it's beautiful,' she said, clamping her hand to her mouth.

The room had the widest bed, tallest ceilings and the best views she'd ever seen. Rose petals had been scattered across the bed, a vase of freshly-cut roses, peonies, carnations and dahlias had been arranged on a glass-topped coffee table and a chilled bottle of champagne was waiting in a bucket of ice. Her father had surpassed himself. It was an incredible wedding gift and the best thing was that she and Victor had the use of it for the entire week.

'Isn't it stunning?' she said, racing around the room. She stopped at the window, pulling back the netting and staring out at the city skyline.

A hotel porter dropped their cases in the corner and withdrew with a courteous bow as Victor slipped him a tip. Ruby threw herself onto the bed with her arms spread wide and almost disappeared into the luxuriously thick bedding.

'What's wrong? You're very quiet. Don't you like it?' she asked when she saw Victor's long face.

'No, it's amazing,' he said, painting on a smile that fell short of his eyes.

He slipped off his jacket, hung it in the closet, and sat on the edge of the bed to loosen the laces of his brogues. Ruby watched him, worried something was wrong. Had she spoken out of turn? Said something to upset him? He'd been so excited on the flight, gripping her hand tightly when she'd screwed her eyes shut as the aircraft took off, the whole plane rattling and shaking like it was about to fall apart. But he'd been quiet since they'd walked into the hotel. Everything about the place was stunningly opulent, from its delicate mosaic tiled floors, grand marble columns and chandeliers hanging from every ceiling to the antique furniture, vases and old books on shelves everywhere you looked. Maybe even a little over the top in its flamboyance, but charming nonetheless. You couldn't help but fall in love with it.

Ruby crawled across the bed and knelt behind her husband, throwing her arms around his strong shoulders and nuzzling her head into his neck.

'I love you, Mr Cano,' she said.

'I love you, Mrs Cano,' he replied.

'Is everything okay? You seem quiet.'

'I'm fine,' Victor said. 'Tired, that's all.'

'If you don't like it, we can find somewhere else to stay. This is lovely, but I really don't care where we are, as long as I'm with you.'

'It's your honeymoon. You deserve to be spoiled.'

And then she understood. Victor's male pride had been dented. 'Think of it as a gift,' she whispered in his ear.

'But it's my job to look after you now,' Victor said. 'I should have arranged the hotel. Not left it to your father.'

'Don't be silly. Just enjoy it. We have our whole lives for you to spoil me.' She giggled.

'But only one honeymoon,' Victor said. 'Come on, let's get some fresh air and see a bit of the city. I don't know about you, but I could do with a drink.'

They spent their first two days drinking negronis in the best bars, sipping espressos under the oppressive heat of the summer sun and overindulging in the finest Italian food. Rome was a vibrant city alive with the buzz of Vespas and chattering young people having fun, and with every cocktail sunk and every plate of pasta cleared, Ruby's happiness swelled like a balloon in her chest.

On their third day, relaxed and finally feeling recovered from the wedding, Ruby dragged Victor to the Pantheon, somewhere she'd always wanted to visit. She suspected he'd have been happy to spend the day lounging in a piazza, watching people over his morning coffee rather than facing the tourist crowds in the stifling heat, but he didn't put up much resistance.

She took his hand and pulled him off the cobbled piazza, under a multi-column Corinthian portico and through tall wooden doors into a cavernous rotunda sitting beneath a spectacular dome, where they stood, hand-in-hand, breathless, awed by the Pantheon's beauty and the sheer engineering achievement.

Inside was cooler, a relief from the relentless heat of the Roman summer and so they took their time, in no hurry to leave, marvelling at the vast checkerboard floor, faded frescoes, classical paintings and larger-than-life statues.

'I could stay here all day,' Ruby said, her eyes gazing upwards, drinking in the architecture. 'It's such an amazing place.'

'It's not fair that one city can have so much history and so many amazing buildings still standing, is it?' Victor said. 'London was so badly bombed in the war, half of it has gone for good.'

Ruby turned a slow circle, taking in all the details. The crowds were swelling, and she took a moment to watch the faces of the people entering the building, their eyes opening wide with wonder, seeing the inside of the church for the first time. Men, women, old, young. It didn't matter. Their reaction was always the same. Awe and wonder.

But as she was watching, a face appeared in the crowds that made her start. At first, she thought she'd been mistaken. Her imagination playing tricks.

'Ruby?' Victor asked as she gripped his hand more tightly, clearly sensing something was wrong.

Ruby edged backwards, her stomach somersaulting and bile rising in her throat.

'No,' she gasped. 'It can't be.'

'Ruby, what is it?' Victor asked, concerned. He turned to look into the sea of faces where she was staring. 'What is it? What's wrong?'

'I need some air,' she said. 'I need to get out of here.'

'Why? I don't understand. What have you seen?'

'It's him,' Ruby hissed, shifting from one foot to the other, agitated. 'He's here. He's followed us.'

'Who?'

'Hugo,' she said. 'Hugo Nightingale is here.'

Chapter 11

A minute passed and Charlie hadn't moved. He continued to stare at me warily, fiddling with his chubby little fingers, his blond fringe hanging over his eyes. I stuck my tongue out and opened my eyes wide like I'd seen other adults do, usually to the amusement of children, but his stony face didn't crack.

'How old are you then, Charlie?' I asked.

Nothing. Just that hard-arsed stare.

'Are you married?' He didn't get the joke.

'Do you go to school yet?'

Finally, a shake of his head. 'No,' he said so quietly I hardly heard him over the noise in the cafe. 'Nurswery.'

'And are you looking forward to seeing your grandparents later?'

I'd lost him again. He said nothing. I glanced hopefully over my shoulder in the direction his mother had disappeared.

'I want my mummy.'

'What?'

'I want my mummy,' he repeated, louder.

A warm flush of panic caused damp patches of sweat under my armpit. 'She'll be back soon,' I said.

'Mummy!' he yelled. 'Where's my mummy?'

'Shhhh!'

A couple at the next table turned around and looked at me anxiously, like they thought I was a child abductor. I shot them a rictus smile.

Charlie's face crumpled and his head flopped onto the table as he wailed, banging his fists, attracting even more attention from people who clearly recognised I had no idea what I was doing.

'Hey, Charlie, come on, don't cry,' I said, reaching for him across the table. 'Your mum'll be back soon.'

He yanked his arm out of my reach and shot me a look of pure hatred, his bottom lip jammed out. He crossed his arms defensively over his T-shirt and almost toppled off the chair.

When I tried to catch him, he wailed even louder. Now everyone in the cafe was looking at us and even people walking past were slowing down to see what was going on.

'I'm just looking after him while his mum's sorting out the baby,' I said to the people at the next table. I looked again forlornly towards the toilets for his mother.

Charlie dropped off the chair and stood by the table, rubbing his eyes, working himself up into a stew. I should never have agreed to look after him. It was well outside of my skill set. Hadn't his mother been able to see that?

'Charlie, sit down,' I said, trying to sound authoritative without shouting.

'Mummy! Mummy! Mummy!' he screamed at the top of his voice, stamping his foot. I couldn't blame him. Dumped by his mother with a complete stranger in an unfamiliar place, no wonder he was panicking.

We were both panicking.

What was I going to do?

'Hey, hey, it's okay,' I said, patting the table to encourage him to sit back down. But he wouldn't come to me.

Instead, he ran off, heading towards a small queue of people waiting to be served. He was surprisingly fast.

I jumped out of my chair. 'Charlie! Come back!' I shouted, but he kept running.

What if he disappeared? How would I explain that to his mother? I'd already lost my wife. It would be unforgivable to lose a child. I started after him as he ducked around the legs of a man staring at his phone.

'Charlie!'

A hand shot out and snatched his arm, stopping him dead and startling him into silence.

A woman who'd been serving behind the counter had grabbed him and was crouching down at his height when I finally caught up with them. She smiled at me sympathetically.

'I thought he was going to run out into the corridor,' she said, holding him tightly by the shoulders. 'Is he yours?'

'No,' I said. 'I'm supposed to be looking after him for ... for a friend. He ran off to look for her.'

'He'll get lost with all these people around,' she said. Like I wasn't aware of that.

'Thanks.' I held out my hand. 'Come on, Sunshine. Let's sit down and wait for your mum.'

'No! Don't want to!' he shouted.

'Hey, what's going on?'

Charlie's mum appeared out of nowhere, smelling of soap and flicking a strand of hair out of her eyes, the baby in the sling wide awake and staring at the ceiling.

'I - ummm ... Charlie got a bit upset,' I said.

'I think he tried to run off to find you,' the woman from behind the counter added. 'Fortunately, I grabbed him before he could escape.'

'Thank you. Thank you so much. Charlie, what have I told you about running off?'

'Sorry,' I said. 'He shot off before I could stop him.'

'Don't worry. It's not your fault. I shouldn't have asked.' Charlie's mother took his hand and pulled him close.

The other woman stood up and shuffled back behind the counter where she'd been preparing a ham and cheese panini, still steaming on a chopping board. 'Hard work at that age, aren't they?' she said.

'Oh my God, he's such a handful. Do you have kids?' Charlie's mum asked in that easy style some people seemed to have when talking to other parents about the tribulations of raising children.

'Two. A little older than yours. They're both at school now. It gets easier.'

'Does it?'

'In some respects. More difficult in others.' She laughed like the other woman had no idea what she had coming.

I felt like a spare part. I didn't know how easy or difficult it was to bring up children. Ruby and I had talked about having a big family, but that was all in the future. I edged away. With Ruby still missing, I didn't have time to stand around chatting about raising kids.

'Where are you going?' Charlie's mother asked, frowning. 'I promised you breakfast in return for some adult company.'

'I'd better get going,' I said.

'You should eat and as you don't have any money, I doubt you're going to get a better offer.'

My stomach rumbled as the woman behind the counter sliced the panini in two with a long bread knife. I was practically drooling as I watched her slip it into a brown paper bag and hand it to a customer.

'Are you sure?'

'Of course, I'm sure. What would you like?'

The woman behind the counter put her hands on her hips and stared at me expectantly.

'Could I have one of those that he had?' I said, pointing to the guy she'd just served.

'Ham and mozzarella panini?'

I nodded with my pulse quickening, trying to keep my eyes from drifting to the crumb-laden chopping board and the promise it held.

The woman turned and opened a fridge, took out a pre-packaged sandwich and dropped it into a hot grill.

'Anything else?'

'A chai latte for me and a hot chocolate for little one,' Charlie's mum said. 'Mr Cano?'

'Call me Victor,' I said. 'Thank you. Nothing for me.'

The woman prepared the hot drinks while my panini cooked and after paying, Charlie's mum headed back to the table.

I waited patiently, hardly daring to believe what I was about to do.

After a couple of minutes, the woman hooked out my panini, dropped it on the chopping board and swiftly cut it in two.

'Actually, could I have a black coffee?' I said.

'Sure.'

She turned her back on me to grab a cup from the stack piled up on a long silver coffee machine behind the counter and busied herself grinding beans.

As soon as she was distracted, I checked over my shoulder, and then swiftly leaned over the counter and grabbed the bread knife. I slid it up my sleeve, along with a blade full of crumbs which scratched my skin like sand.

I glanced across at Charlie and his mum. She was trying to persuade him to sit down and drink his hot chocolate. It was now or never. I stepped away from the counter and strode purposefully out of the cafe into the corridor.

'Hey! Sir? You've forgotten your panini!' The woman called after me.

But I kept my head down and disappeared into the crowd. Just a guy on a mission. No one was going to help me. If I was going to save Ruby, I had to take matters into my own hands.

Chapter 12

'Where?' Victor asked, his chest puffing up and his hands balling into fists.

But when Ruby looked again, Hugo had vanished. She was sure she hadn't imagined seeing him. She'd spotted him in a slow-moving queue of people shuffling into the building. His eyes had locked onto hers with no hint of surprise, like he'd known she was inside. Like he'd followed her. But now he'd gone.

'Over there,' she pointed towards the entrance, breathless.

'Are you sure?'

'Yes, I'm sure. Oh my God, what's he doing here?'

The last time she'd seen him, he was being manhandled out of her parents' garden after gatecrashing their wedding reception, drunk. Her father promised he'd got the message that she wasn't interested. She was married to Victor now, and she loved him more than anything and anyone. To follow her to Rome, on her honeymoon, was so creepy. What did he think he was playing at?

'Want me to have a word with him?' Victor asked.

Ruby had a sense that if Victor found him, he'd likely do more than just have a quiet word. And who could blame him?

Ruby shook her head. 'No,' she said, grasping Victor's chest. He wrapped an arm around her waist and pulled her possessively close. 'Let's just get out of here.'

'I don't understand why he's here,' Victor said. 'Are you sure you're not just seeing things?'

'It was him! Please, can we go?'

'Alright.' Victor took her by the hand. They threaded their way through the hordes of visitors and spilled out into the mid-morning heat.

Victor checked they weren't being followed and then whisked Ruby away, through the Piazza della Rotonda, towards the river, scurrying with furtive glances over their shoulders, until Ruby insisted they slow down.

'Wait,' she gasped. She stopped and clutched her side, her face glowing.

Victor peered back the way they'd come. 'It's okay,' he said. 'I can't see anyone. If he was here, we lost him.'

'I need a drink.'

They found a cafe with tables overlooking a circle of wooden huts selling newspapers, books and antiquities and ordered espressos and limoncellos, sitting nervously on the edge of their seats, watching everyone who walked past with suspicion.

'What do you think he wants?' Victor asked, taking Ruby's hand and straightening her diamond solitaire engagement ring with his thumb.

'He's lost his mind.' Ruby shook her head sadly. 'I think he still hopes there's a chance we'll get back together.'

'I can't believe he's followed you here on your honeymoon. The guy's deranged.'

Ruby wished she'd never set eyes on him. At first, she'd been flattered that someone as ennobled as Hugo Nightingale was interested in someone like her. But she realised now what a big mistake she'd made. She'd made it plain that she had no feelings for him, but still he wouldn't leave her alone. No, that wasn't true. She did have feelings for him. They were feelings of hatred and disgust. She despised him. And sitting at that cafe, with fear threading through her veins, she wished him dead.

'I'm sorry,' she said.

'What? No, this isn't your fault.' The skin around Victor's kind, beautiful eyes creased.

'I thought Daddy's people had spoken to him when he crashed the wedding.'

'The problem is people like Hugo Nightingale aren't used to being told what to do. They don't like it.' Victor scratched his chin as he glanced over his shoulder for the twentieth time since they'd sat down. 'As soon as we get home, I'll speak to your father and see if there's any more he can do.'

Ruby finished her coffee and washed it down with the glass of chilled limoncello.

'How do you think he knew where we were going to be?' she asked, running her finger around the rim of her cup, wiping away the dried crust of crema.

'I have no idea.' Victor shook his head.

'What if he booked into the same hotel and followed us this morning?' Ruby said, swallowing hard.

Victor froze, his eyes growing wide. 'The same hotel?'

Ruby shrugged. 'Daddy was telling anyone who'd listen where he'd booked for us. It wasn't a secret. What if Hugo found out and decided to come after me?'

'No, he wouldn't have, would he?'

'I wouldn't put anything past him.'

'Oh my God,' Victor said. 'That's the craziest thing I've ever heard.'

'There's only one way to be sure.' Ruby stood up suddenly. 'Come on. Let's go. I need to know.'

Two hours later, and still determined to confirm whether Hugo had been so bold as to book into the same hotel, they returned to the St Regis and approached a pretty blonde woman with prominent cheek bones and a smart French plait who greeted them with a welcoming smile at the reception desk.

'Good morning,' she said in perfect English.

'We've arranged to meet a friend here later,' Ruby said. 'Could you let me know if he's checked in yet?'

The smile on the receptionist's face didn't move an inch, like it was permanently drawn on. 'What was the name?'

'Nightingale,' Ruby said. 'Hugo Nightingale.'

The receptionist checked the hotel register. 'Mr Hugo Nightingale? Yes, he checked in last night. Would you like to leave a message for him?'

'Great,' Ruby said, feigning pleasure, hiding the bilious wave of nausea rising from her stomach. 'I'd like to surprise him. He's a very good friend of ours. I don't suppose you could let me know his room number?'

The receptionist's smile finally slipped a little, her eyes narrowing. 'I'm afraid we don't usually -'

'It's been years since we've all seen each other. I can't imagine his face when he sees us again,' Ruby continued, faking a laugh. 'He won't believe it!'

'I can get a message to him?'

'A few of us arranged to meet up in Rome to celebrate his birthday, you see. It's a big one.'

'I'm not really allowed to -'

'Please?' Ruby pressed. 'It's his thirtieth.'

The receptionist stared at Ruby for a second or two, looking awkward. Ruby said nothing, leaving the weight of pressure on the other woman to fill the silence.

'Room three one four.'

'Three one four,' Ruby repeated. 'Thank you so much.'

She snatched Victor's arm, and they hurried towards the elevators.

'I knew it,' she hissed. 'He's here.'

'Okay, so what now?'

'I'm going to speak to him,' Ruby said, with a steely determination in her eye.

'No, I don't want you going near him.'

'I have to, Victor. I have to make him understand it's over. I can't live looking over my shoulder for evermore, wondering if he's watching. I'm going to tell him once and for all that I'm not interested.'

'Let me go. I'll speak to him.'

Ruby stopped abruptly. 'He won't listen to you, and besides, you'd probably end up punching him. Go back to the room and wait for me. I won't be long.'

'Ruby -'

'Please, Victor, do as I ask. I'm going to deal with this.' She handed him the room key.

He stood biting his lip for a moment, not moving, but eventually threw up his arms in defeat.

'Fine. Ten minutes. And then I'm coming to find you,' he said.

'I love you.' She stood on tiptoes to kiss him.

'Please be careful.'

'I will.'

They rode the elevator together in silence, and on the third floor, Ruby stepped out. She watched the doors close and Victor, his face stone cold, disappear. She took a deep breath and walked the corridor, counting off the rooms until she found room three one four.

She had no idea what she was going to say. She only knew she had to make Hugo come to his senses. She didn't love him. She never had. He had to let her go so they could both get on with their lives.

She raised her hand and knocked on the door.

She heard movement in the room. Footsteps. Hugo flung the door open, his face the picture of surprise.

'Ruby,' he said. The sick smile that crept across his lips made her want to retch. 'Come in.'

He stepped aside, but Ruby stayed where she was.

'What the hell are you doing here? This is madness,' she said.

'I've come for you.' Hugo's brow creased, as if it wasn't obvious.

'Hugo, I'm married! You've followed me on my honeymoon.'

'But I love you,' he said.

'Enough! Stop it! I don't love you, Hugo. I love Victor. He's the man I married. He's the man I'm going to spend the rest of my life with. You were … a mistake.'

Hugo looked wounded. 'Don't say that.'

'It's true. I was flattered you showed interest in me, but only because you're a viscount. We have nothing in common.'

'This man you married -'

'Victor.'

'What is he? A company director? He's not good enough for you. He can't provide for you like I can. Come with me, Ruby. It's not too late for us to be together.'

Ruby shook her head, tears of anger and frustration pricking her eyes. 'No, Hugo, you're not listening. I don't want to be anywhere near you.'

'You don't mean it.'

'I do,' she hissed.

'Give it time. You'll learn to love me as much as I love you.'

'You're not listening,' Ruby said. 'There is nothing between us and there never will be. I'm warning you, Hugo, leave me alone.'

'I can't.'

'You know who my father is, don't you?'

He stared at her, silently, and for the first time he looked worried.

'Yeah, that's right,' Ruby said. Finally, she had him on the back foot. 'If I tell Daddy what you've done, that you're stalking me, you know he'll fix it, don't you?'

Hugo swallowed hard.

'Permanently. He's an influential man and he can make people like you disappear.' She snapped her fingers. 'Just like that. Gone in a puff of smoke. One word to Daddy and he'll see you never bother me again.'

'Ruby -'

'I mean it, Hugo, leave me and Victor alone or you'll regret it.'

Chapter 13

It was now or never. There was no point sitting around thinking about it. I needed to act before the woman in the cafe raised the alarm. My lips and throat were desert dry and my pulse fluttered like a butterfly's wings as I pushed and barged past anyone in my way, my focus entirely on reaching Ruby.

I descended the stairs onto the concourse slowly, holding the handrail with an iron-like grip, wary of falling with a knife up my sleeve. Safely on the ground floor, I took a steadying breath before heading for the arrivals gate where a semi-circle of people were fanned out, waiting for the next planeload of passengers.

I stood next to a man in a crisp white shirt and dark waistcoat who was holding up a cardboard sign with the name of someone he was meeting scribbled on it in black ink. He looked like a limo driver. He smiled and nodded. To anyone watching, I was just another friend, father, husband, uncle, brother or taxi driver waiting to greet a traveller returning home.

I waited. Nervous. Determined. One door on the glass security tunnels swung open and a white-haired man in a garish Hawaiian shirt and a woman I took to be his wife emerged pushing a trolley stacked with cases, their skin tanned from a holiday in the sun. It heralded the arrival of a fresh flush of passengers.

Still I waited, shuffling my feet anxiously as I let the knife slip out of my sleeve and into the palm of my sweat-slick hand, concealed on the inside of my arm.

Next to emerge were a younger couple with two school-aged children. They strode purposefully into the arrivals hall, blinking under the disinterested gaze of the people watching. More people came through in twos and threes, small groups, mostly families.

Then I noticed a group of twenty-something women approaching the gates, chatting and giggling with casual ease, all with healthy tans and long hair bleached by the sun, probably back from celebrating a hen party or a birthday. Or a group of university students who'd organised a couple of weeks away together. It didn't matter where they'd been or where they were going, only that they were a larger group coming through the gates together. It was what I'd been waiting for.

Folding doors hissed open and they stepped into one of the glass security tunnels one at a time, walking in single file, dragging cases on wheels. I counted the first woman's eight short strides it took her to walk the length of the tunnel. She was blonde, wearing a short denim skirt and her arm a colourful riot of woven bracelets. She hesitated only briefly as the door at the far end of the tunnel, nearest to where I was standing, popped open and folded back on itself, allowing her to exit.

At the other end, two of her friends were still queuing to enter, leaving doors at both ends wide open. It was the best opportunity I was going to get. I rushed towards the woman in the denim skirt, pushing her out of the way, trusting everyone would be too shocked to stop me.

'Move!' I yelled as I encountered a second woman exiting the tunnel. I grabbed her arm and yanked her out as I charged in.

She stumbled and screamed, but I wasn't deterred.

Two more women from the same group inside the tunnel froze when they saw me rushing towards them with the knife.

'Get out of the way!' I yelled, barging them to one side, aiming for the far door, still open.

I stumbled over one of their cases and nearly fell, but sheer bloody will and determination kept me on my feet. A stale breeze hit me in the face as I rushed towards the open door. So close. I reached out, confident now I was going to make it.

But suddenly, a strip of green lights on the floor turned red, an earsplitting alarm sounded and the doors snapped closed. I slipped my fingers through the rubber seal between them and tried to force them open, but they were locked firmly shut and wouldn't budge an inch.

In a terrified panic, I turned and ran back, but found the door at the other end of the tunnel had also slammed shut, trapping me inside with the two women. Like a caged tiger, I prowled up and down, trying to work out how I could escape, while an automated female voice warned me to remain calm and that someone would attend shortly. How stupid I'd been. I was snared like a mouse in a trap, with no way out.

The two women cowered together in a corner, clutching each other, their eyes fixed on the bread knife in my hand.

'Shut up,' I snapped when they started whimpering. I waved the knife in their faces. I needed to think.

'Please don't hurt us,' one woman pleaded.

'I'm not going to hurt you. But you need to keep quiet. I need to think.'

She nodded vigorously.

The alarm was so loud. A deafening siren that rattled around my head. And my heart was racing so fast I thought it was going to tear itself out of my chest. I had to do something.

A flash of movement outside caught my eye. The two police officers who'd been pursuing me earlier ran towards the glass tunnel with their semi-automatic rifles raised and grim expressions on their faces.

'Drop the weapon!' one of them screamed at me, aiming his gun through the glass.

I froze and he started yelling again. 'Drop the weapon and get down on the floor!'

Two more armed officers with guns came charging towards me from the opposite end of the airport, so now I had the barrels of four rifles aimed at my head. But I figured I still had the upper hand while I was behind the glass with the two women.

'Come here,' I hissed at one of them. She was a pale, mousy-haired, skinny waif with multiple piercings in her ear.

'What?' She gawped at me like I was some kind of monster.

'Come here,' I repeated, grabbing her arm and pulling her to me.

She screamed but didn't put up much of a fight when I reminded her I was holding a knife. I don't know what I was doing or thinking, but I wrapped an arm around her neck and held the knife to her bare skin.

'Let me out of here or I'll cut her throat,' I heard myself shouting at the officers through the glass.

'Drop the weapon! Don't do anything stupid!' they continued to yell at me.

My head was spinning. My legs weak. My breath came in short gasps from my tight chest. Hands sweating. Everything was going wrong. I'd lost Ruby and now I was holding a woman at knifepoint, surrounded by armed police. How the hell had it come to this?

'Let me out of here,' I hollered. 'Open the doors!'

'We can't do that until you let the girl go and put your weapon down,' the police officer said, calmer now. He used his hand, palm facing down, to indicate he wanted me to get on the floor.

'I just want to find my wife,' I wailed, emotion choking the words in my throat. 'I just want to find Ruby.'

I let my arms relax and the knife fell away from the skinny woman's throat. She wriggled free from my grasp and scurried back to her friend as I collapsed to my knees in tears.

'Put the knife down, Sir.' At least the officer had stopped yelling.

The alarm cut off and the flashing red lights went out. At last I could hear myself think. I dropped my head in my hands as uncontrolled sobs racked my body. What the hell would Ruby think if she saw me like this?

'The knife, Sir. Please throw it to one side.'

I lifted it in front of my face and stared at the serrated blade. What had I been thinking? This wasn't me. I'd never hurt anyone in my life. How had it come to this, trapped in an airport security tunnel with two hostages and a knife? I was desperate, but this was stupid. Someone was going to get hurt, and Ruby would never thank me for that.

I threw the knife away. It clattered against the glass and fell to the floor. I could almost feel the relief radiating off the four police officers, all of them frozen in a firing stance with their guns aimed at me.

'Good,' the officer nearest to me said. 'Now slowly, on your stomach and put your hands behind your head.'

I breathed in through my nose and glanced at the two women hugging each other, pressed up against the glass as if they were trying to get as far away from me as possible.

'I'm sorry,' I said. 'I didn't mean to scare you. They took my wife away. I was only trying to find her. Please forgive me.'

With tears trailing down my cheeks, I rolled over onto my chest and put my arms behind my back.

The four officers split into two pairs, one set moving to the entry doors, the other to the exit. I heard a click and a buzz and both sets of doors sprang open.

They pulled the two women out to safety first and I squeezed my eyes tightly shut as an officer knelt at my side, pushed my head roughly into the ground and snapped a pair of handcuffs onto my wrists.

Chapter 14

They drove me away in the back of a squad car, still handcuffed, to a nearby police station for questioning. They were obviously keen to get on with it as I wasn't held in a cell for long after being processed by a tough-looking custody sergeant who read me my rights and reminded me I'd been arrested on suspicion of terrorism offences. I stifled a laugh, not sure how anyone could interpret what I'd done in desperation as an act of terrorism. All I'd wanted was to find Ruby, but I guess it was all part of the game the police were playing. Hit me with a serious charge and try to break me. But if they thought I was going to make their lives easy, they could think again. Unless they told me what they'd done with Ruby, I wouldn't cooperate. They'd offered to appoint a lawyer on my behalf, but I figured I'd be better off representing myself. And besides, I didn't trust lawyers.

I waited for a few minutes on my own in a bare, windowless interview room before two detectives strode in and pulled up chairs on the opposite side of a scuffed wooden table. A woman in a plain white blouse buttoned up to her neck and long, dark hair pulled back into a severe ponytail led the questioning. An older guy with grey hair, a lined face and a charcoal suit sat at her side, mostly silent. She introduced herself as a detective sergeant and said her name was Villiers. The guy was more senior. A detective inspector called Paul Metcalfe. I didn't like the woman's face or the way she looked at me. She had a rat-like pointed nose, sharp cheekbones and an unpleasant sneer. Ruby would have said she looked as hard as nails. A real ball breaker. Well, I was ready for her.

'Mr Cano, perhaps you could start by telling us why you were at the airport?' Villiers asked, folding her hands on the table.

I took a deep breath and let it out slowly. I considered keeping silent. Whatever they thought I was guilty of, it was up to them to prove it. No need for me to help them out. But then I remembered they had caught me red-handed with a knife in a secure area, holding two women hostage. Maybe it would be better if I cooperated to see where they were going with it. They might even tell me what they'd done with Ruby.

'I was looking for my wife,' I said. 'We flew back from our honeymoon in Rome yesterday evening, but ...' I hesitated. 'I lost her.'

I watched Villiers' face carefully. She knew as well as I did Ruby hadn't gone missing. They had detained her when we'd landed for some reason I hadn't yet worked out.

'What's your wife's name?'

'Ruby,' I said. 'But you already know that, don't you?'

Villiers frowned. 'What makes you say that, Mr Cano?'

So, she wanted to play games. I sat back and folded my arms, saying nothing.

Villiers shook her head when I didn't reply and referred briefly to a sheet of paper in a cardboard folder on the table. 'Can you tell us when you last saw your wife?'

Was that supposed to be a trick question? She couldn't possibly know that I couldn't remember anything about the flight home. I had to tread carefully. 'I woke up in the arrivals hall this morning and she was gone,' I said, skirting the question.

'That's not what I asked. When did you last see your wife?'

I flushed hot and cold, panic rising. 'I guess on the plane home,' I said.

'You guess?'

'On the plane.'

'Right, so somewhere between landing and disembarking from your flight, you lost her?'

'I - I ...' I stammered. 'I don't know. My memory is a little hazy. We must have become separated inside the airport after we landed.'

'I see,' Villiers said.

I had the sense she was testing me, seeing if I'd lie to her. She knew exactly what had happened to Ruby. I bet she had it written on that piece of paper, angled so I couldn't read it.

'I don't remember exactly,' I said. 'I think I hit my head.' I pointed to the wound on my temple, which had finally stopped bleeding and was scabbing over. 'I don't remember much about the last twenty-four hours, but I assume something happened after we landed. I'm pretty sure she must have been detained by the police or customs or something. But you'd know more about that than me.'

'Why would you think that?' She continued to stare, her gaze boring through me.

'Because what other explanation could there be?'

Villiers consulted her sheet of paper again. 'And when you became separated, you decided to stay the night at the airport?'

'I told you, all I can remember is waking up there this morning. Please, if you know what's happened to my wife, tell me,' I pleaded. 'I can't bear not knowing.'

'A routine police patrol spotted you earlier this morning after they were alerted by a member of the public concerned that you needed medical attention. Why did you run from them when they challenged you?'

I shrugged.

'Because, you see, that raises all kinds of red flags to someone like me, especially when it happens inside an airport. Can you see that?'

'I suppose,' I said, sounding like a petulant teenager.

'Why did you do it?'

'I don't know.'

'Were you worried that they'd discover you were carrying a knife?'

'I wasn't carrying a knife,' I said. 'Not at that point.'

'So you acquired the knife later?'

'I stole it from a cafe.'

'I see,' Villiers said. 'So why didn't you stop when asked to by the police patrol?'

I ran my tongue over my teeth. She must have known full well that they were looking for me, even though I had no idea why. Of course I was going to run, at least until I'd worked out what had happened to Ruby. 'I was confused.'

'Confused?'

'I didn't know what had happened to my wife. I thought she was in trouble and that they were coming after me next.'

'So you had a guilty conscience. Why would that be, Mr Cano?'

She was twisting it. 'I just had a bad feeling in my gut.'

'A feeling in your gut?' She scribbled a note on the piece of paper. 'Tell me about the knife.'

'I told you, I stole it from a cafe.'

'Why?'

'I thought I might need it,' I said.

'In what way?'

'Because I knew I had to get into the other side of the airport to find Ruby. I thought it would help and so when I saw it lying on the counter, I took it.'

'A spur-of-the-moment decision?'

'Yes.'

'But your plan was to take a hostage?' she asked.

'No!'

'The two women you threatened were pretty traumatised,' Villiers said.

'I'm sorry. I didn't mean to hurt anyone. I panicked.'

Villiers tapped her pen against her front teeth. The noise set my nerves on edge. I wished she'd stop. 'How old are you, Mr Cano?'

'What?'

'It's a simple question. What's your age?'

'Twenty-eight,' I said. 'What's that got to do with anything?'

Villiers and Metcalfe exchanged a glance.

'And you were returning from your honeymoon, you say?'

'That's right.'

'How was it?' she asked, with an unexpected smile curling on her lips, no doubt trying to unsettle me by suddenly coming over all friendly.

'I'm sorry?'

'How was your honeymoon? Did you have a good time?'

'Yes,' I said. 'It was perfect. Why?'

'No arguments?'

'No.'

'No cross words?'

What was she trying to suggest? 'No,' I said. 'We had the most amazing week. Neither of us wanted it to end. We were very happy.'

'Hmmm.'

What did that mean? Didn't she believe me? Oh God. Did she think I'd hurt Ruby? Was she trying to frame me?

'I didn't do anything to her, if that's what you think,' I said.

She smiled again, but this time there was no warmth in her eyes.

'When you were detained, you weren't carrying any identification. No passport. No driver's licence. No money. No credit cards. You didn't even have a wallet,' Villiers said.

'That's right.'

'Can you explain why? If you'd recently arrived back in the country, you should have had your passport with you.'

'I think I was mugged.' It was the only plausible explanation I could think of. 'It would explain this.' I tapped my temple again, turning my head slightly to show her the wound.

'Any idea where or by whom?'

'No. I don't remember it happening.'

'That's convenient,' Villiers said.

'Not for me.'

'No, I suppose not.'

'How did you get to the airport?'

I shook my head as I tried to think. 'I - I must have driven,' I said.

'You don't remember?'

'No,' I said, frowning. I had a vague recollection of packing up our cases in the back of my car after the wedding. 'Actually yes,' I said, as the memory of leaving the car at a large open air car park at the airport came back to me. It had been a sunny day, and we'd driven with the roof down and the wind in our hair. Yes, that was right. I remembered now.

Villiers opened her mouth to ask me another question but was interrupted by a knock on the door. It opened a crack, and a man stuck his head through the gap.

'Sarge, can I have a quick word?'

She looked annoyed but nodded and suspended the interview while she stepped out of the room.

I was left alone with the detective inspector, but he didn't even look at me. He continued writing notes on a pad of paper, his lips pursed and his legs crossed.

A minute later, Villiers returned. She slipped the male detective a piece of paper and sat down.

'For the benefit of the recording, DS Villiers has returned to the room,' she said. She pulled her chair closer to the table and leaned in towards me.

The bad feeling in the pit of my stomach was back. Whatever information she'd just been handed, I sensed it wasn't good news.

'Mr Cano,' she said, grim-faced. 'We've run some checks on the information you've given us.'

'Okay.'

'Why have you been lying to us?'

'What? I haven't,' I said, confused.

'Please, it's time to drop the act.'

'What act?' My stomach lurched and roiled.

As Villiers spoke, I had the sensation of the walls closing in on me from all four sides, forcing the air out of the room. What she was saying made little sense.

'We've checked with all the airlines and Border Force,' she said. 'No one with your name or your wife's name has been on any flight in the last week to or from Rome.' She raised both eyebrows, her eyes opening wide. 'In fact, they have no record of anyone with your names being on any flights to anywhere at all.'

Chapter 15

They left me to stew in a claustrophobic cell for a few hours while they made further enquiries, but it was obvious DS Villiers was convinced I'd been lying to them. They must have made a mistake. Maybe they'd misspelled my name. It happened all the time. Cano wasn't a common surname. I'd inherited it from my father, who'd moved to Britain from Spain when he met my mother, and even though they'd later divorced and she'd remarried, I'd kept it. It had been too much fuss and paperwork to change it.

I sat on the edge of a thin plastic mattress on a concrete ledge that was supposed to pass as a bed and chewed my nails down to the tips of my fingers as I tried to puzzle out what the hell was going on.

There were only two possibilities. Either there had been a mistake and the airline had an incorrect record of our flights. Or there was some kind of cover-up going on. But who would do that and why? The police? Immigration? The security services? Maybe it had something to do with

Ruby's father. It was an open secret that Sir Nigel was a senior figure in MI5. Maybe even the top man. He kept the precise details of his position close to his chest. But what reason would he have to engineer Ruby's disappearance and have our names scrubbed from the flight manifest?

Something to do with Hugo Nightingale, then? Ruby's ex-boyfriend had made himself a real nuisance after they'd split up. Not only had he shown up drunk at our wedding, but he'd followed us to Rome on our honeymoon. I didn't see him, but Ruby was adamant she'd spotted him in the Pantheon, and the hotel confirmed he'd booked a room two floors below ours. Ruby was so incensed she'd confronted him against my better judgement. We thought whatever she'd said to him had done the trick. We never saw him again.

Had we been naïve to think that would be the end of it, though? Hugo's father was the Earl of Ruttingham, for God's sake, and that entitled toff was used to getting whatever he wanted. What if he'd taken exception to the humiliating way Ruby had treated him and done something stupid? It was an extraordinary idea, but everything in the last twenty-four hours seemed warped and twisted.

No matter which way I turned and bent the facts, I couldn't make sense of it, and I was grateful when they finally hauled me out of the cell and marched me back into the interview room. I couldn't stand to be left alone with my own thoughts any longer.

Villiers and Metcalfe were already sitting at the table, but I immediately noticed a difference in their demeanour. They seemed less hostile. Less threatening. Villiers' eyes even creased when she smiled and asked me to take a seat.

'What is it?' I asked. 'Have you found her?'

'Please, Mr Cano, sit down,' she said.

I knew then that something bad had happened. They felt sorry for me. I could read it in their faces. That could only mean one thing.

'Oh my God, is she —?' I couldn't bring myself to say it. I pulled out the chair and slumped down, defeated. 'Hurt?'

Villiers glanced down at her hands, her fingers laced together on the table. 'There's someone here to see you,' she said. 'But this might be difficult for you.'

'Ruby?' I gasped. Had they found her at last? Brought her to the station? 'Is she okay?'

Villiers raised a hand to stop me. 'It's not Ruby.' She hesitated for a beat. 'It's your son, Patrick.'

'What?'

She stared at me without blinking, working her jaw while she waited for me to process the information.

'Patrick? I don't understand. We don't have any children.'

'He's been worried about you, Victor.'

What happened to Mr Cano? I shook my head in disbelief. They were trying to mess with my head. They'd taken Ruby and now they were trying to break me with this crazy talk.

'I don't know anyone called Patrick. Why are you saying these things?'

'Take it easy, Victor. I'm going to bring him in now and you can have a chat.'

'I don't want you to bring him in. I want to know what's happened to Ruby.' I slapped my palm on the table. 'Why aren't you taking her disappearance more seriously? You should be ashamed of yourselves.'

Villiers closed her eyes for a second, waiting for me to calm down, and then stood. She walked to the door and disappeared out of the room.

'What's going on?' I said, leaning towards Metcalfe. He still hadn't said much, even though he was supposed to be the senior officer.

'Things will become a lot clearer when you've spoken to Patrick,' he said. He had that same sad, sympathetic look in his eye as Villiers.

'Please, just tell me what's going on.'

'Everything's going to be okay, Victor. You're in good hands now.' He talked to me like I was a child.

The door clicked open. Villiers returned with another man. He stepped in, blinking at the surroundings, tugging at two loose drawstrings that hung from his top, unzipped over a distended beer belly. He looked a little older than me. Maybe mid to late forties, not totally bald, but the little hair he had left arched over the top of his head like a hirsute bridge from one ear to the other, making his forehead seem unnaturally large.

'Hello, Dad,' he said, his face lighting up when he saw me.

I recoiled at his familiarity, although he looked vaguely recognisable, like I'd seen him in a film once, a long time ago.

'Who are you?'

'Take a seat.' Villiers grabbed a chair and placed it next to me.

The man approached it cautiously, pulled it back a little farther away from me, and sat.

'What have you got yourself into now, Dad?' he said, shaking his head, his eyes rimmed red like he was holding back tears.

I glanced at Villiers and Metcalfe for an explanation, but they were both sitting back, arms folded, observing silently.

'Who are you?' I demanded.

'I'm Patrick,' the man said. 'Your son. Don't you remember?'

'I don't have a son.' My lungs constricted as if someone was sitting on my chest.

The man swiped a tear from his cheek with his thumb. 'You have two sons,' he said. 'Matthew is in Australia. We haven't seen him in a while, but we've both been worried about you.'

I shook my head, trying to expel his words from my ears. Why was he saying these things? It was absurd. The guy was at least twenty years older than me, for a start.

'I'm sorry,' I said. 'I don't know who you are or why you're pretending to be my son.'

The man bowed his head and sniffed.

'I'm sure you're only trying to help,' I added, feeling bad that he was getting upset, but he'd clearly mistaken me for someone else.

'Dad, please,' he begged. 'Try to remember.'

'I don't know what you're talking about.' What kind of hell was this? Were they deliberately trying to make me question my sanity? 'All I'm interested in is finding my wife. I need to find Ruby.'

'Dad!' the man said. 'Listen to me.'

He'd turned his chair so he was facing me, leaning forwards with his arms resting on his knees.

'Do *you* know where Ruby is?' I said, angrily, 'because if you don't, I don't know what you're doing here.'

'I'm really sorry, Dad. I didn't want to have to tell you like this, but Ruby's dead.'

Chapter 16

'Aren't you tired yet?' Victor asked playfully as Ruby finished her glass of champagne and grabbed him by the hand, pulling him onto the dance floor.

The room was swaying with people and thick with cigarette smoke that hung under the ceiling like London smog.

'One more dance and then we'll leave,' she said, her head swirling with the buzz of alcohol.

The negronis and champagne had flowed as freely as tap water after they'd eaten and found themselves in the Via Veneto, dodging hordes of paparazzi loitering outside the bars, cafes and nightclubs, hoping to catch a glimpse of a famous face.

Victor pretended to haul himself reluctantly from his seat, rolling his eyes in mock exasperation, allowing himself to be led onto the dance floor with the throb of the band ringing in his ears. He pulled Ruby close, their bodies pressing together, moving in perfect sync. They fitted together so naturally, it was as if they'd been made for each other. A marriage designed in heaven.

'This is the best honeymoon I've ever had,' Victor said, his smile growing wider as Ruby punched him on the arm.

'I hope it's your only honeymoon.' She raised an eyebrow and laughed.

And without a care for what anyone else in the club thought, he kissed her full on the lips, a long, lingering kiss full of promise and the expectation that their evening was far from over.

Eventually, with their feet aching and their eyes stinging, they threaded their way out of the club, the air outside still heavy with the residual heat of the day.

'I don't want to go home,' Ruby said as she skipped along at Victor's side, twirling and quick-stepping to the music still playing in her head. 'It's been the most wonderful week of my life.'

'You'll always have the memories,' he said. 'And we'll be back. We should make it an anniversary tradition.'

'Yes, let's!' Ruby cried. 'Let's come back every five years until we're old and wrinkly.'

Victor threw his head back and laughed, his eyes narrowing and his broad chest heaving. Ruby couldn't imagine what it would be like when they were old. She pictured them with grandchildren running around their feet, their hair white and their skin liver-spotted and leathery.

'Every five years? Are you sure?' he said.

'Of course, I'm sure. I'm in love with Rome, didn't you know?'

'I thought you were in love with me?'

She put a finger to her lips, as if she was thinking. 'You come a close second,' she said, giggling.

'Hey!' He tried to grab her, but she ran off, skipping ahead towards the Piazza Barberini.

He eventually caught her as she trotted over a crossing, weaving between a buzzing convoy of scooters and onto the cobblestones that formed a stone island in the middle of a sea of beautiful, regal buildings.

'Dance with me,' she said, snatching his hand and throwing her face up towards the stars in a cloudless sky.

He took her in his arms and twirled her around and around as if they were still in the club and the band had struck up a song just for them. Their last few hours in Rome. In the morning, they'd be heading back to England to start their new life as a married couple. Ruby couldn't wait to tell Yolanda all about Italy. The amazing food they'd eaten. The breath-taking ancient architecture. The stunning hotel where they'd been treated to every luxury imaginable. And how Hugo had almost ruined everything turning up and booking a room at the St Regis.

Ruby pictured Yolanda's reaction when she told her how she'd spotted him in the crowds at the Pantheon. She'd be appalled. They'd not seen Hugo again after she'd had a word with him, warning him off. She assumed he'd checked out and returned home. Hopefully, her message had been received loud and clear and it was the last they'd see of him. She was in love with Victor and they were going to live a long and happy life together. And there was no place for Hugo.

When Ruby spotted the Fontana del Tritone and the clear blue water lapping around the heads of four limestone dolphins supporting Triton on their tails, she couldn't help herself. She kicked off her heels and, hitching up the hem of her little black dress, climbed in, squealing with delight as the water reached her knees.

'Come on in, it's lovely,' she said, holding out her hand to Victor, urging him to join her.

He laughed and shook his head, picking up her abandoned shoes. 'I don't think you're supposed to paddle in there,' he said.

She pouted. 'I'm not doing any harm.' She bent down and splashed water at him.

It showered his face and dampened his shirt. 'Watch it!'

'Or what?' She laughed again as she threw more water in his direction.

'Ruby, stop!'

He charged, pretending to chase her. She screamed and turned, wading through the water to the other side of the fountain. But he was quicker, darting around a low barrier supposed to stop people climbing in as she clambered out. Laughing so hard she could hardly breathe, Ruby backed away from him.

'You're in big trouble now,' he said, raising his arms and growling like a monster.

Ruby screamed again, then turned and ran, padding across the cobbles in her bare feet, leaving wet footprints in her wake.

'I'm coming for you,' he said, as she reached the edge of the raised island surrounded by a road, busy with taxis and Vespas even at that late hour.

She turned to face him, edging away. 'No, please,' she giggled.

He lunged for her and she bolted.

Straight into the road. Without looking.

A squeal of tyres ripped through the heart of the night.

A dull sickening thud as Ruby's body collided with a speeding taxi, knocking her off her feet.

She collapsed in the street, oblivious to the broken bones and ripped skin as the shock of the impact rendered her body numb.

All she could think about was her dress. The fabulous little black dress Victor had bought for her as a gift.

Was it ruined?

'Ruby!' Victor was at her side, holding her head. Her hand.

The look on his face told her it was bad. She couldn't move, but the pain was otherworldly, like it belonged to someone else.

'I'm sorry,' she whispered.

'You're going to be alright. It's going to be okay.' Victor was virtually hyperventilating. 'For God's sake, someone call an ambulance.'

But she knew it was too late.

She'd hit her head as she'd fallen and the dark edges at the periphery of her vision were closing in, like she was staring at Victor's face through a long telescope.

'Stay with me, Ruby.' He threw his jacket over her trembling body and brushed the hair out of her eyes. 'Don't you dare leave me,' he kept repeating.

He was crying now. Thick, heavy tears dripping down his cheeks and off his chin. She was vaguely aware of a crowd gathering. Faces looking down at her.

'I've had the best week of my life,' she said, struggling with the breath to speak, a nasty gurgling sound bubbling up from her chest.

'We'll be back,' Victor sobbed. 'Every five years, remember? Until we're old and grey.'

'I love you, Mr Cano,' she mouthed, not sure if the words had come out.

'I love you, Mrs Cano. I'll always love you.'

She was being dragged away. Disappearing into a dark, lonely place.

'Ruby! Ruby!' Victor was screaming now. Frantic.

But his voice drifted away as the darkness enveloped her soul.

And finally silence and peace and a glowing white light arrived to carry her away.

Chapter 17

Patrick yanked a belt over my shoulder and strapped me into the front seat of his car, buckling me up like I was an invalid, incapable of doing anything for myself. I was numb and confused, still reeling from the shock that Ruby was dead, I was an old man and that I had a family I couldn't even remember. I felt myself shrinking away, recoiling from the world like a tortoise retracting into its shell.

As Patrick pulled away, leaving the grey police station behind, I watched out of the window as trees and hedges swept past in a blur of olive and sage, not sure what I was supposed to be thinking or feeling.

'You okay, Dad?' Patrick asked, resting his hand on top of mine momentarily before changing gear.

His skin was warm and soft, but it was like being touched by a stranger.

'What?' I murmured, my voice croaky and weak. An old man's voice. Tired and spent.

I watched him, my son, as he drove, looking for evidence of the truth he wanted me to believe, in the hook of his nose, the colour of his eyes and the cut of his jaw. I couldn't see any of Ruby in him at all, but I recognised the curl of his lip when he smiled. My lips. My smile.

'It's not far,' Patrick said. 'The nurses will be pleased to see you. They'll make sure you're comfortable.'

'Nurses?'

Where the hell was he taking me? To the hospital? I wasn't ill.

'At the home, Dad, remember? Ivy Lodge. It's where you live now. They're really nice there.'

Ivy Lodge? The name meant nothing to me.

A plane growled loudly above us. It appeared suddenly ahead, frighteningly close, skirting over the road and dipping out of view behind a hedge as it came in to land dangerously low, its jet engines whining.

No wonder I couldn't remember the flight home with Ruby. She hadn't been with me. I must have flown home alone, dazed and distraught, trying to comprehend the death of my bride. A lump forced its way into my throat, making it hard to swallow, and my eyes moistened with tears. How could I have forgotten something as traumatic as the sudden death of my wife on our honeymoon?

'What I can't understand,' Patrick said, taking his eyes off the road to glance at me briefly, 'is how you got to the airport.'

I wasn't sure myself, although I had a vague recollection of handing over a fistful of coins on a bus and stumbling to a seat by a window.

I shrugged.

'Or how you got out of Ivy Lodge with no one noticing.'

What did it matter? It was such an insignificant detail in the wider scheme of things. I'd just discovered my wife, the woman I adored, had died less than a week after we'd married, I had two middle-aged sons, and apparently I now lived in a nursing home because I was no longer capable of living by myself.

'And what did you do to your head?'

'I fell,' I said.

I'd thought I must have been mugged, and they'd taken my money and my jacket, but now I wasn't so sure. I'd fallen at least twice since I'd woken up in the airport, tripping over Stan's trolley and then stumbling down the stairs as I tried to run from the police. I wasn't as steady on my feet as I'd thought.

After a fifteen-minute drive, Patrick pulled up in a car park outside a red-brick lodge with a dull grey tiled roof and white plastic windows. It was the sort of anonymous-looking building you'd pass without a second glance.

Patrick ratcheted on the handbrake, killed the engine and slipped off his belt.

'Here we go,' he said. 'Home sweet home.'

It didn't look like home to me. Home was where the heart was, and my heart was still with Ruby.

A fine drizzle had begun to fall, misting the windscreen as grey clouds gathered overhead. I stared at the grim building with a dark sense of foreboding. It definitely wasn't home. It's where Patrick had brought me to die, surrounded by the sick and the infirm. A waiting room ahead of the final reckoning. Only a few hours ago, I'd been convinced I was still in my late twenties, full of life and vigour, and in the blink of an eye, I'd aged sixty years. I was an old man. My life done. My memories fading.

Patrick helped me from the car, my old bones aching and stiff, like I'd never known before. I could hardly walk. My feet shuffled slowly, supported under one arm by Patrick. A woman with straggly long blonde hair streaked with grey and wearing a shapeless nurse's uniform over black leggings came rushing out of a set of automatic sliding doors which whispered open.

'Victor!' she said, clearly pleased to see me from the grin on her face. 'You had us all worried sick. Where have you been, you silly sausage?'

'Hi, Sylvia,' Patrick said. 'One patient returned safe and sound.'

Sylvia took over from Patrick, helping me inside. Stale coffee and tobacco on her breath, and a rasping smoker's cough and yellowing teeth.

'Hello, Victor,' someone called out from behind a reception desk. A young woman I didn't know. 'Good to have you back.'

I waved a trembling hand, noticing how old and wrinkled my skin appeared.

I managed the stairs slowly, gripping tightly to the handrail, and reached the first floor a little out of breath. The interior of the building was light and airy, and all the walls were painted white to reflect the light. But a lick of paint couldn't disguise the smell. It was the smell of the slow creep of death - boiled vegetables and urine-saturated mattresses. I shuddered.

Sylvia led me into a bright room with a window overlooking a cherry tree in the back garden. It was a pleasant enough space where I recognised my books on the shelves and my tweed jacket hanging on the back of a chair. A faded black-and-white photo of Ruby and me on our wedding day was in a frame on a chest of drawers.

'There you go,' Sylvia said, letting go of my arm. 'I'll leave you two to get settled in. Give me a shout if you need anything.'

Patrick shot her a kindly smile and pushed the door closed. I collapsed in the armchair by the window and ran a craggy hand over my face. What now?

Patrick hovered, fizzing with tension, and finally sat on the edge of the bed. He looked tired.

'You really don't remember anything?' he said.

I shook my head. My head was full of Ruby. The day she'd stepped out in front of my car, and I took her to lunch to apologise, feeling like I'd met my soulmate. And I could remember every detail of our wedding day, the lace and pearl trim on Ruby's dress, the colour of the flowers that decorated the church and the speech I stumbled over at the reception. It was as clear in my mind as if it had been yesterday. But everything after Rome was a hazy shadow.

'I'm sorry,' I mumbled. I could see how much it hurt Patrick that my memories were gone. Memories of his childhood. Memories of our life together.

When he saw my gaze on the photo taken the day Ruby and I married, he stood and handed it to me. I took it in trembling hands and held it up to my face. We were standing in the church door, speckled sunlight dappling through the leaves of an old oak tree, our smiles as wide as oceans. We looked so happy. Our whole lives ahead of us. Or so we thought.

'I wish I'd had the chance to meet her,' Patrick said.

'You'd have liked her very much. Everyone did.'

'I'm sorry, Dad. I really am.'

I squeezed my eyes shut as the last moments of Ruby's life finally came back to me. Dancing around the Fontana del Tritone in the Piazza Barberini and Ruby running barefoot into the road. The taxi driver who stood no chance. Holding Ruby's hand as her eyes fluttered closed one final time.

Patrick returned the photo to the chest of drawers and picked up another in a plain white frame. He gave it to me and sat back on the bed, watching my face.

Another wedding photo. A man who looked like me was wearing a dark suit with ridiculously wide lapels and hair that covered his ears. Next to him stood a bride in a white, long-sleeved flowing dress holding a bouquet of dahlias. A stirring of recognition awakened in my mind.

'Do you recognise it?' Patrick asked.

I gulped. 'Yes.'

'That's you and Mum on your wedding day.'

I looked up at Patrick, willing the memories to sharpen into focus.

'She's beautiful,' I said. Unlike Ruby, she was dark-haired and round-faced. Her eyes shone with joy.

'Do you remember her name?'

I plumbed the depths of my mind, fishing for it. It was there somewhere, just under the surface, but out of reach. Frustration bubbled through my veins. Why couldn't I remember?

'Grace,' Patrick said, putting me out of my misery.

'Grace,' I repeated, running my thumb over her face.

'You had a wonderful marriage. You were very happy.'

I shook my head, confused. 'What's wrong with me, Patrick?'

'What do you mean, Dad?'

'Why can't I remember?' I said, choking on my tears.

Patrick bowed his head and his shoulders slumped. 'Dementia. It's affecting your brain. There's nothing they can do.'

'Nothing?'

Patrick pinched the top of his nose and sobbed. 'No,' he said.

'It's okay.' I patted his hand. 'Don't get upset. Tell me about your mum.'

'Your wife.'

'Yes, tell me all about Grace.'

'You were married for forty-five years,' Patrick said.

'Forty-five years?' Ruby and I had been married for only a week before she died. A mere blip compared to nearly five decades I'd been married to Grace.

'And you had two sons. Me, of course, and Matthew. He's in Australia now. He's an electrical engineer.'

I nodded, but I couldn't recall his face.

'And Grace? Where is she?'

Patrick took a deep breath. 'She's gone, Dad,' he said, his eyes flooding with tears.

'I don't understand.'

'Breast cancer. I'm sorry.'

'She's dead?'

'Five years ago.'

It was another body blow. In the space of a few hours, I'd effectively lost two wives. A sadness swelled in my chest. Maybe it was better I couldn't remember.

Patrick reached under the bed, pulled out a cardboard box and plucked out an album filled with photographs in plastic sleeves. He opened it on my lap and flicked through the pages for me. It was full of pictures of a family I couldn't remember. Happy, smiling faces. Love. Laughter. Joy. The four of us on the beach. Christmases around sparkly trees. Walks in the forest. Birthdays. Football in the garden. Trips to foreign cities. Barbecues under a hazy sun. A whole life I'd forgotten I'd ever lived. Treasured memories captured forever on film.

When he'd finished, Patrick sniffed and closed the album. He took it from me and traced his finger over its front cover.

'Thank you,' I said. 'I enjoyed looking at the photos.' I didn't tell him I didn't remember any of it. How could I? It would have broken his heart.

He wiped the back of his hand across his cheeks, swiping away the tears, and smiled. 'Would you like me to take you to see Mum?' he said.

'See her?'

'I mean her grave. I could pick you up tomorrow and take you there, if you'd like.'

'Yes,' I said.

'We could take flowers.'

'Is it far?' I asked.

'Only a few minutes down the road, by the train station. Why don't I pick you up at ten?'

'Yes, please,' I said. 'I'd like that very much.'

Chapter 18

Patrick finally left when I feigned tiredness and told him I needed to sleep. Actually, I needed some space to think and I couldn't do that with him loitering around, fussing over me.

He took some persuading that I was fine to be left and when he was gone, I picked up the photo album he'd left on the bed and went through every picture, looking for a memory. Something I could remember, even at the corner of my mind. I focused on the grinning faces. My two boys. Matthew, the older one, looked a lot like me. Patrick looked more like his mother. They had the same nose and even tilted their heads in the same way, slightly to the left, when they laughed. And Grace. My wife of more than forty years. How tragic that we'd been together for so long and I couldn't recall anything about her. She must have been the woman who put me back together after Ruby's death and made me appreciate that life was worth living, even in grief. I wondered how we'd met. Maybe she'd known Ruby. A friend, perhaps? A confidante?

It was hard to believe that she was the woman whose face I'd woken up to every morning for almost half a century and who'd given me two sons. The disease in my brain had robbed me of it all. I couldn't remember any of it and yet every detail of my brief life with Ruby was as clear as if it happened yesterday. My cheeks burned with shame. Ruby might have been my first true love, but Grace had been the woman I'd shared my life with.

I found four more albums in the box under the bed and went through every photo, piecing my old life back together, trying to rebuild the memories I'd lost. It was the least I could do for Grace's sake. And for Matthew and Patrick. They deserved a father who remembered them.

As I flicked through the pages, my eyes grew heavy. It had been a long and exhausting day, but I wouldn't let myself sleep. If I drifted off, who knows what memories I'd have left. Would I wake convinced Ruby was alive again and with no recollection of my family? Would I have to relive Ruby's death all over, like some macabre Groundhog Day? I couldn't take that risk and so I forced myself to stay awake.

I put the photo albums back where I'd found them in the box under the bed and sat in the chair by the window clutching the two framed pictures of my two weddings and my two wives.

And I came to a decision.

At six o'clock, one of the nurses came to my room and took me to a dining hall on the ground floor, where I sat at a table with five strangers and ate a stodgy and insipid meal in silence.

I spent the rest of the evening in my room thinking, convincing myself I could remember more than I could. I needed to do it for Patrick and for Matthew and, most of all, for Grace. At nine, Sylvia came to put me to bed. She helped me into a pair of thick cotton pyjamas and held my arm as I slipped under the sheets.

'Goodnight, Victor,' she said, turning out my light. 'And no more midnight excursions, please. Your son would never forgive us if we let you out of our sight again.'

I closed my eyes, pretending to sleep, but as I heard her footsteps padding along the hall, I sat up and switched on the bedside light. By ten, the building had fallen silent.

I pulled on my trousers and shirt over my pyjamas, grabbed my jacket and cracked open the door. I sneaked along the empty corridor and down the stairs. There was no one behind the reception desk and, to my astonishment, the entrance doors slid open as I approached. I slipped out into the darkness, buttoning up my jacket, and headed down the drive towards the main road. I was expecting someone to stop me at any moment. Someone calling my name. A hand on my shoulder. But it didn't happen. Someone would probably get into trouble for leaving the entrance unlocked, but that wasn't my problem. All I was concerned about was reaching the cemetery.

I couldn't wait for Patrick to collect me the next morning and risk losing all my memories again. I needed to reach Grace while she was still fresh in my mind. For all I knew, the dementia rotting my brain could snatch her away at any moment.

I reached the road and hesitated as a stream of fast-moving cars buzzed past. Patrick had said the cemetery was near the train station, which I recalled seeing on our way to Ivy Lodge. It was one of the few things I could remember clearly. That and the embarrassment of being told by the female detective that I was being released pending further enquiries. I think they wanted some time to consider what to do with me. I'd admitted stealing a knife and using it to force my way into a security tunnel plus taking a woman hostage, but the state of my mental health was a complicating factor, I'd heard the detective telling Patrick.

I turned right and shuffled as quickly as I could along the pavement until I saw the bright lights of the train station ahead. People loitering around outside, smoking. A line of taxis waiting for fares. The rumble of a train in the distance. Opposite the station, I spotted the cemetery, set back behind wrought-iron railings and bushy yew trees. But a sign on the gates, which were padlocked shut with a heavy chain, revealed it was only open during daylight hours. I peered through the bars into the darkness beyond. A path forked off in two directions, meandering into the distance between crooked headstones. But there was no way in, other than climbing the gates, and even if I had still been in my twenties, that would have been a mean feat.

Maybe there was a gap in the fence further along the road. I shuffled on a short distance, feeling the chill of the night penetrating my bones. At least it wasn't raining. But the fence and the yew trees went on as far as my eye could see. Tall and foreboding. No way inside. It was hopeless.

I slumped to the ground and sat on the freezing pavement with my back against a low stone wall. It hadn't occurred to me that I wouldn't be able to get into the cemetery at night. My teeth chattered. At least it was too cold to sleep. I wrapped my arms around my body for warmth and lowered my head onto my creaking knees, my only choice to stay until the gates opened in the morning, and hope no one discovered I was missing from Ivy Lodge before then.

'Hey, pal, you alright?'

I looked up into the glassy eyes of a man with a dirty face and a ripped jacket who was swaying on the spot, clutching a can of strong lager. His Glaswegian accent was almost impenetrably strong.

'I'm fine. Thank you,' I mumbled between chattering teeth.

'You look cold. Are you lost?'

'Not exactly,' I said.

The man threw a smelly blanket he had over his shoulder onto the ground and sat on it next to me. He offered me his can of beer. I shook my head. He took another mouthful and belched.

'People call me Beam.' He stuck out a hand to shake.

It was warm and calloused, and he had a firm grip.

'Beam? That's a strange name.'

'You know, like the bourbon. Jim Beam?'

'Right,' I said. 'Victor Cano.'

'I've not seen yous around here before,' Beam said.

I wasn't sure how much to tell him. Would he raise the alarm if I explained that I'd run away from Ivy Lodge? Probably not. We were all running away from something.

'My family put me into a nursing home,' I said.

'Oh, aye.' The man pulled out a rolled up cigarette from a breast pocket in his shirt and lit it with a plastic lighter. He took a deep drag and blew out the smoke in a plume before offering it to me.

'No, thank you,' I said.

'So you've run away?'

'I came to visit my wife's grave but the cemetery's shut.' I pointed over my shoulder.

'Aye.'

I remembered the framed photo I'd shoved into my jacket pocket before I'd walked out of the home. I pulled it out and showed it to Beam.

'That's my wife, Grace,' I said.

'She's a good-looking gal.'

'She died of cancer.'

Beam nodded as he studied the photo.

'This sounds terrible, but I can't remember anything about my second wife or my sons,' I said, a niggling claw of guilt scratching at my insides.

'I wish I could'a forgotten ma wife,' Beam said with a chesty laugh.

'My son offered to bring me to see her grave tomorrow, but I'm worried that if I sleep, I'll have forgotten about her by the morning. I don't know what to do.'

'You got any cash?' Beam asked. 'I'm starving.' He finished his beer, crushed the can and tossed it down the pavement. It skittered into the gutter in the road.

'Sorry, no,' I said, patting my jacket pockets and realising I'd forgotten to pick up my wallet.

'Nay problem.'

'Sorry,' I repeated. He was stick thin and unhealthily pale. I wondered when he'd last eaten. I would have offered to buy him something if I'd brought any money. I wanted to ask him how he'd ended up on the streets, but I thought it would be rude to quiz him.

'You know you can get in round the back through Joyce Street?' Beam said.

'Into the cemetery?'

'Yeah, there's a missing fence panel behind the back of the garages.'

'Can you show me?'

Beam licked his lips and pulled a strand of tobacco from between his teeth. 'It'll cost you,' he said, his eyes narrowing.

'Oh,' I said. 'I don't have any money.'

'I'm kidding, you crazy old bastard.' Beam laughed out loud and prodded me in the arm. 'It's a joke.'

He jumped up with surprising energy and tossed the blanket over his shoulder. 'Come on then,' he said, reaching for my hand to pull me up. 'What are you waiting for?'

'Thank you,' I said, my muscles protesting stiffly as I got to my feet.

I struggled to match Beam's stride as he marched off, staggering drunkenly and shouting obscenities at random passing cars.

'Keep up, old man,' he called over his shoulder.

When he turned into a dark alleyway behind a row of houses, I hesitated, not sure if I was doing the right thing putting all my trust in a homeless drunk who might be luring me off the beaten path to kill me, for all I knew. But I couldn't wait on the street all night for the cemetery to open. My only chance of getting inside to see Grace's grave one last time was to follow him.

'You coming or what?' he yelled.

I dug my hands into my trouser pockets. 'Yeah, I'm right behind you,' I said.

Chapter 19

A loud hammering on the door startled Patrick awake. He checked his phone. Just gone seven. Too early for visitors or the post.

'Who's that?' his wife groaned, rolling over.

'I don't know.' Patrick sat up and rubbed his eyes, his heart pounding.

He grabbed a T-shirt from the end of the bed, pulled it on and staggered down the stairs to the door.

Two serious-looking police officers were standing outside with expressions that hinted it was bad news. Patrick's legs jellied. He gripped the door frame for support.

'Patrick Cano?' the first officer asked, while his colleague stared at the ground, unable to meet his eye.

'Is it Dad?' he said, with a tremor in his voice.

'Can we come in?'

Patrick stood to one side with his pulse galloping. 'What is it? Has he run off again?'

'May we sit down?' the first officer, a man with unusually light hazel eyes and dark skin, asked.

Patrick showed them into the lounge. The two officers sat next to each other on the edge of the sofa while he took the armchair by the TV, his mind in turmoil.

'I'm afraid it's not good news.' Hazel Eyes put his cap in his lap and rested his hands on top of it.

Patrick tried to swallow, but his throat was too dry. 'What's happened?'

'I'm afraid your father was found dead this morning.'

'Dead? I only saw him last night. He was fine. I don't understand,' Patrick stammered.

His wife appeared in the door, tying up her dressing gown, her hair all mussed up. 'What's going on?'

'It's Dad. He's ... dead.' Even as he spoke the words, they didn't seem real. How could his father have died? He might have been losing his mind and struggling to walk on stiff legs lately, but otherwise, he'd been in good health.

'He was found at the cemetery near the nursing home this morning,' Hazel Eyes said, while his colleague continued to look as if he'd rather be anywhere but in their home breaking bad news.

'The cemetery?'

'We understand he lived at the Ivy Lodge Nursing Home? It appears he walked to the cemetery last night and somehow found a way inside. The gates are locked at six, so it's not clear how at the moment, but we are checking CCTV footage to confirm.'

Patrick shook his head, trying to take it all in. 'They let him walk out again?'

The officer frowned. 'How do you mean, Sir?'

'He walked out two nights ago and somehow got himself to Gatwick Airport, looking for his first wife.' Patrick buried his head in his hands. 'They promised me it couldn't happen again.'

'His first wife, Sir?'

'He has dementia. In the last few days, he'd not been able to remember anything other than her. It's crazy. He was only married to her for less than a week before she died.'

'I'm sorry to hear that.'

'The home was supposed to be keeping a closer eye on him,' Patrick said, his anger building, furious with the staff. How could they have let this happen? He'd trusted them.

The two police officers glanced at each other. And then Hazel Eyes checked his notebook. 'He was found by his wife's grave,' he said, glancing up at Patrick. 'Grace Cano?'

'Yes, that's my mother. His second wife.'

'He was discovered by the caretaker, who raised the alarm at around five this morning. An ambulance was called, but I'm afraid he was declared dead at the scene. I'm very sorry.'

'How did he die?'

'That's not clear yet. There'll be a post-mortem examination because of the circumstances, but there's nothing to suggest there was any foul play.' The officer hesitated for a second and put his notebook down. 'It was cold last night and Mr Cano was found wearing only a thin jacket.'

'I see,' Patrick said, fuming. What the hell was the home playing at, letting his father escape for a second time in twenty-four hours? They wouldn't hear the end of this. His father was dead, and it was because of their negligence. They were paying enough to keep him at Ivy Lodge. The least he should have expected was that his father would be safe under their care.

'If it's any consolation, I was told he looked at peace,' Hazel Eyes said. 'He didn't suffer.'

'Thank you.'

The second officer finally looked up and caught Patrick's eye. He had something in his hand Patrick hadn't noticed. 'He was clutching this when they found him,' he said, handing it to Patrick. 'We thought you'd like to have it.'

Patrick wiped a finger across the glass, removing a smudge of dirt. It was the picture of his mother and his father on their wedding day, looking like the happiest couple alive.

A tear pricked Patrick's eye and suddenly he began to sob uncontrollably.

They buried Victor with Grace in the cemetery where he'd died, finally reunited in the ground after forty-five years of blissful marriage. The police briefly flirted with the idea that Victor may have been attacked before his death, after discovering security camera footage from the train station showing him chatting and walking off with a homeless man. But Victor's body showed no signs of any physical assault, and when they traced the man, who called himself Jim Beam, he'd protested he'd only been trying to help Victor find his wife's grave because he felt sorry for the old man.

A post-mortem concluded that hypothermia caused Victor's death. He'd spent the night out in the open, underdressed, exposed to the elements, and his frail, aged body couldn't cope with the cold. The sad conclusion everyone reached was that Victor had simply taken himself off to die.

Patrick's brother, Matthew, flew back from Australia for the funeral, a low-key ceremony held in a small church near to Ivy Lodge. His father had stipulated he wanted little fuss. Immediate family only, which limited it to Patrick and his wife, and Matthew, whose girlfriend hadn't been able to take time off work to fly to Britain to be with him.

Matthew stayed for a few days after the funeral to help sort through Victor's room. They'd already cleared out most of his belongings when they'd sold his house to fund his care, and there wasn't much left after that. A few books, a wardrobe of old clothes and some personal effects. He hadn't needed or wanted much in his later years, when his brain and memory began to deteriorate. Patrick kept the photo albums and Matthew held on to his father's military medals from his brief time in the army. The rest was bagged up and taken to a charity shop.

Patrick also kept the framed photograph from his father's doomed first wedding to Ruby, and on the day that would have been their fifty-fifth anniversary, he made a pilgrimage to the church in Buckinghamshire where they were wed.

It was a beautiful July day with wisps of woolly clouds floating high in an azure sky, which showed off the church with its towering steeple in its most glorious splendour.

He found the grave in the north-eastern corner of the churchyard, under the shade of a mighty oak tree in full leaf, and half hidden under a healthy crop of nettles, although someone had clearly visited recently. A narrow path had been trampled through the weeds and a single red rose deposited under the headstone. Patrick had no idea who might have been there before him. He understood Ruby's parents had lived in the village, but they would surely be long dead, and as far as he was aware, she had no brothers or sisters.

He shrugged and put it out of his mind. Probably one of the villagers who remembered her and laid flowers every year. He stamped down the worst of the nettles, brushed off some of the moss that had collected on the headstone with his thumb and laid his own flowers. He'd also brought roses. A dozen of them. Ruby red. It felt fitting. He laid them on the narrow rectangle of grass he'd cleared and sat for a minute in quiet reflection, wondering what might have been if Ruby had survived.

In those lucid moments, after he'd returned his father to Ivy Lodge, Victor had told him the whole sad story about Ruby's death. It was weird to think that in that split second when she'd run into the road at the precise moment a taxi was passing, Patrick's entire existence had been determined. If Ruby had lived, if she'd never stepped into the road, the chances were his father would never have met Grace, and Patrick and his brother would never have been born. A sliding door moment of epic significance.

The strength of his father's love for Ruby was clear. He'd remembered her even when the dementia had robbed him of his memories of Grace, returning to the airport in the forlorn hope of finding her sixty years after her death. At first, it had upset Patrick that his father had no recollection of his sons, until he reminded himself the disease attacking his brain was to blame. It didn't mean he loved Grace or Patrick or Matthew any less. Dementia was a nasty, filthy, indiscriminate disease that wrecked families and destroyed everything in its path. And yet, amid his father's mental disintegration, he'd remembered Ruby and that she had needed him. He couldn't remember why, only that as a devoted husband, it was his loyal duty to save her. And there was something inherently romantic about that. A pinprick of light in a dark storm. In his final hours, it was Patrick's mother, Grace, his father had returned to. It was heartbreaking, but at least now his father was at rest. He'd not defeated the disease, but he'd been able to choose how and where to die. And that was something of comfort.

Patrick stood up and stretched his back. Time to get going. It was a long drive back around the M25 and he'd promised his wife he'd be back for dinner. He took one last look at Ruby's grave and the roses he'd left. Next time he'd remember to bring a brush and give the headstone a proper clean. He'd do it for his father, in honour of the first, but not the last, love of his life. And as he backed away, he read the inscription on the headstone one last time, with a sad smile and a nod to the woman his father never forgot.

Ruby Cano
Loving wife, taken too soon
14th November 1944 - 23rd July 1967
Her absence a silent grief. Her life a beautiful
memory.

ALSO BY THE AUTHOR

HIS WIFE'S SISTER

He stole her childhood. Now she wants it back.

Mara Sitwell was only a child when she went missing nineteen years ago. Now she's been found alive and well, wandering barefoot and confused in remote woods.

She tells investigators she was imprisoned in an underground cell – but refuses to reveal anything about her abductor.

Her brother-in-law, Damian, doesn't think her story adds up. He's convinced she's dangerous - and a threat to his young family.

To protect them, he'll have to prove what really happened to her all those years ago - even if Mara's not ready to give up all her secrets just yet...

AVAILABLE FROM AMAZON

SHE KNOWS

Some secrets are worth dying for...

Esme and her husband, Frank, had everything they could have wanted – until they lost it all and took refuge in a quiet island town where no one knows their secret.
On the same island, Sky is trying to rebuild her life and her self-esteem after her mother's brutal death.

But following a chance encounter between the two women, Sky becomes convinced Esme is in mortal danger and vows to do everything she can to help.

The last thing Esme needs is someone poking their nose in her business. But Sky won't take no for an answer.

She sees it as the chance to redeem the wrongs of her past - even after she finds herself caught up in something far bigger than she could ever have imagined and accused of a murder she has no memory of committing...

AVAILABLE FROM AMAZON

BETWEEN THE LIES

The perfect girlfriend – or a perfect stranger?

Jez thought he'd finally found happiness when he met Alice. She's elegant, stylish and beautiful, the kind of woman he never imagined would look at him twice.

But when Alice goes missing with her young daughter and the police accuse him of their murders, his life is shattered.

The only way to prove his innocence is to find them alive. But that's not so easy when Alice is running from a grim family secret - and she doesn't want to be found...

AVAILABLE FROM AMAZON

Printed in Great Britain
by Amazon